Reasons to Be Happy

"Gripping! I was instantly swept away by Hannah's struggles and greatly inspired by her journey. This is a powerful book, and I recommend it for anyone who has ever worried about how to fit in."

—Kristina McBride, author of *The Tension of Opposites*

"Reason to be happy number 303: Reading this book. Seriously. Katrina Kittle masterfully nails the angst, insecurity and confusion of the world of eighth grade. A must-read for anyone who ever tried to fit in."

—Sharon M. Draper, *New York Times* bestselling author of *Out of My Mind* and other books for teens

Reasons to Be Happy

Katrina Kittle

 sourcebooks
jabberwocky

Published by Sourcebooks Jabberwocky, an imprint of Sourcebooks, Inc.
P.O. Box 4410, Naperville, Illinois 60567-4410
(630) 961-3900
Fax: (630) 961-2168
www.jabberwockykids.com

Library of Congress Cataloging-in-Publication Data
Kittle, Katrina.
  Reasons to be happy / Katrina Kittle.
    p. cm.
  Summary: Eighth-grader Hannah Carlisle feels unattractive compared to her movie star parents and cliquish Beverly Hills classmates, and when her mother's cancer worsens and her father starts drinking heavily, Hannah's grief and anger turn into bulimia, which only her aunt, a documentary filmmaker, understands.
  [1. Bulimia—Fiction. 2. Grief—Fiction. 3. Schools—Fiction. 4. Popularity—Fiction. 5. Self-acceptance—Fiction. 6. Beauty, Personal—Fiction. 7. Ghana—Fiction.] I. Title.
  PZ7.K67157Re 2011
  [Fic]—dc23

                              2011020276

                    Printed and bound in Canada.
                    WC 10 9 8 7 6 5 4 3 2

For Rachel Moulton,
talented writer and beautiful friend,
who is always a reason to be happy,
as are the following, especially when shared with her:
good coffee, dark chocolate, salted caramel,
Jeni's ice cream, Gerbera daisies,
and zombie movies.

Chapter 1

Reasons to Be Happy:

1. Swimming with dolphins
2. Outrunning a forest fire
3. A hot air balloon ride
4. Seeing a shark fin while surfing but making it back to the shore intact
5. Hiking by moonlight

I used to be brave.

What happened to the girl who wrote those things? The girl who left the house that morning all excited about her first day of eighth grade at a new school? That girl who got up way too early and flipped through her sequined purple notebook where she keeps a list of things that are good in life—things like:

20. The smell of Band-Aids
21. Cat purr vibrating through your skin
22. Hiking with Dad up on Arroyo Seco and seeing a mountain lion at dusk
23. Vampires
24. Playing with the rubbery residue after you let glue dry on your fingers

How could so much change so fast in just one day?

Scratch that. Stupid question. Besides, it wasn't really a day. It was a summer. How could they change so fast over one summer? Let's see, you could move to a new school, be totally humiliated, have no real friends, and oh, yeah, your mom could get cancer.

Yep, that about does it. That would explain the changes. So, the harder question is: how do I get that girl back? That girl who saw so many reasons to be happy that she started to keep a list:

6. Making lists
7. Jumping on a trampoline in the rain
8. Ghost stories
9. Painting your toenails
10. Winning a race

11. Dark chocolate melting in your mouth
12. Pad Thai so spicy hot it makes your nose run

I missed that girl. She used to be bold and fun. Then she became a big chicken loser. "There goes Hannah," Aunt Izzy used to say (okay, her name is really Isabelle but everyone calls her Izzy), "jumping in with both feet."

Aunt Izzy is my mom's sister. She lives in Ohio (where she and my mom grew up) in a funky purple house in this hippie town called Yellow Springs (*Aunt Izzy's purple house* is reason #28 on the list). Aunt Izzy makes documentary films. I know, I know, documentary films sound boring, but she makes *good ones*. Her last one won an Academy Award. My mom and dad are actors. They've never won Academy Awards, even though both of them have been nominated. They make their living in feature films, which is why we live all the way in Los Angeles now.

Aunt Izzy said I "jumped in with both feet" like it was a compliment, like it was good and brave. (Which reminds me, *running hurdles when you hit your stride just right* is #56.) My mom, though, said I jump in with both feet like it's a very, very bad thing. "You don't have any fear," she said with this look of exasperation. But that was before I became afraid of everything. I hesitated too long before I jumped. I waited, paralyzed, thinking of all the bad things that could happen, until the moment was gone. It was like, once I stopped risking, I lost the ability.

Like that day, my disaster of a first day—I hesitated too long. I let the wrong things gain momentum and there was no way to stop the avalanche.

Chapter 2

Reasons to Be Happy:

70. The smell of Play-Doh
71. Sand under your bare feet
72. Seeing a shooting star
73. Riding the front car of a roller coaster
74. Raw cookie dough
75. Glitter

These were some of the things I listed before I turned into a big loser.

In my journal that morning (which is different from the purple Reasons to Be Happy book) I listed all the things I would do at my new school:

1. Make at least three new friends

2. Join track team

3. Sit with a different group at lunch every day. Get to know everybody!

4. Take more art classes

Oh my God. Who *was* that girl? I wrote those dorky, cheerful things and I really believed they would work.

I told you my parents were actors, but did I mention that they're...unnaturally gorgeous people? They've turned heads all their lives, even before they were famous. People just like to look at them, the same way they like to gaze at lovely flower arrangements or trees in bloom in springtime.

My dad filled a room, and not just with his broad-shouldered height. People breathed easier around him; I'd seen it happen. Something about those muscled arms, those high cheekbones, and those really long lashes (totally unfair to waste on a man, if you ask me) all added up to this casual, comfortable *certainty*. He made you feel safe, like he'd handle anything that threatened you, just like he did in his movies. His teeth could hypnotize you, lighting up a room like a flashbulb. Really, that wasn't an exaggeration; his face would be all still and listening, then *flash!* off went that smile. You felt like you'd been touched by the sun when it was aimed at you.

It hadn't been aimed at me in a long time.

Seeing my mother made people stop and say "oh" aloud, like they'd seen the Taj Mahal or a perfect sunset—even while she was so skinny and sick. She liked to say, "Pretty is as pretty does," and it was truer of her than of anyone else I'd ever met. When she was healthy, her pale, porcelain skin glowed like moonlight against her paprika hair. She had kind, hazel cat eyes and a pixie nose that turned up slightly at the bottom. Her smile was slower than my dad's; it started in the corners of her mouth (where she has these great dimples) then slowly unfurled. She crinkled her nose when she smiled or laughed. Everyone—men and women alike—smiled back, looking grateful, like they'd been handed a gift.

So with breeding like mine, I should've been hot, right? What happened? I was as tall as my dad, which meant I towered over everyone in my grade. I wasn't petite like Mom at all. I was this ogre that got switched at the hospital. I was sure there was some big, ugly, giant couple somewhere with this pretty, proportioned, ballerina-looking girl just giving each other high-fives every day.

I always knew I wasn't as beautiful as my parents, but you know what? I never knew I was *ugly* until I showed up at my new school.

I liked my old school. I liked school in general. But Mom and Dad had both gotten new attention in bigger, critically acclaimed roles and had become worthy of paparazzi. We hadn't had to deal with that before. I mean, occasionally a fan would stop one of them in a coffee shop or at a gas station or whatever, but with my dad's last movie, *Cold Right Hand*, people were taking our pictures when we went to pick up Thai food or shopped for toilet paper.

So over the summer, they had enrolled me at a private school that had security especially for this reason.

Everything might've been different if Brooke hadn't been my "host" that day.

When Brooke called me the day before, she was so friendly I felt like I was in great hands. Maybe I should've been clued in by the way she gushed, "Caleb Carlisle is really your *dad*? Oh my *God*, that must be so cool. You are so, *so* lucky."

Probably half of the kids' parents at my new school work in the film industry (and a bunch of the kids are actors themselves), but Brooke's dad was CEO of some bank.

Brooke's eyes narrowed when I walked up the school sidewalk. She looked me up and down in a way that made me feel naked.

I wore my usual jeans, T-shirt, and flip-flops. My hair was in a ponytail. I wore no makeup. I reached up and touched my earlobes—nope, I hadn't put in any earrings.

Brooke had on jeans too, but stylish jeans embroidered with sequins and flowers up one thigh—one very *skinny* thigh, that is. She wore strappy sandals with heels and a see-through gauzy top with a pin-tucked camisole underneath. She had on not only earrings, but a necklace, bracelet, and rings on most of her manicured fingers and even on one toe. Her dark hair was piled up loosely on top of her head, like she was going to an awards show.

She looked like a woman.

I looked like a little girl.

A chubby, plain little girl.

"Hannah?" she asked, like there might be a chance she was wrong.

I nodded.

"Okay, then," she said, throwing back her shoulders. "Come on." She pulled me into a bathroom and offered me some makeup. I hardly knew what to do with it, so she took it out of my hands to apply it herself. "You'll wanna ditch the backpack and wear better shoes," she said.

I almost laughed and said, "I don't remember asking your opinion." Why *didn't* I? The Hannah I'd been that morning when I'd left my house would have. Why didn't I say, "no thanks" to the makeup? Why did I let her take down my ponytail, and fluff up my hair and spray it?

Was it the way the other pretty girls squealed her name and kissed her on the cheek? Was it the way a girl—a plain girl, like me (named Kelly I later found out)—stepped into the restroom then turned right back around and left when she saw Brooke with her friends?

"Don't talk to her," Brooke said when the girl was gone.

Brooke's friends, Brittany and Bebe (pronounced bee-bee, like the gun, or the stinging insect, both of which are appropriate), both hyperventilated over my dad. They fell all over themselves with questions. What was he like? Was he funny? Did we have a pool? Where did he work out? What was he filming now? Did I know how lucky I was?

"What's your name again?" Brittany asked me. Brittany looked almost identical to Brooke except she had *blond* hair piled on her head instead of dark. But she also wore tight jeans, a camisole, and filmy shirt.

"Hannah," Brooke answered for me, combing my hair. "Hannah Anne Carlisle. Isn't that, like, so…*Midwest?*"

She said Midwest like it was dog crap.

"My mom's from Ohio," I said, closing my eyes against the sting of hair spray.

"We know," Brooke said. She quoted the tabloid line in a singsong voice. "'From farm girl to starlet.' I wouldn't brag about that."

Bitter hair spray filled my open mouth.

"Annabeth Anderson," Brittany recited my mother's name. "Talk about Midwest. That's a hick name, really."

"But she looked awesome in *Tinfoil Butterfly*," Bebe said. Her tone implied that looking awesome kind of made up for the name. Bebe was African American but was in the same "uniform" as Brooke and Brittany. Even her black hair was piled up in those ringlets.

"Any of your parents act?" I asked.

They all snorted. Brittany's parents were both plastic surgeons. Bebe's dad was a cardiologist. Her mom was an oncologist.

"Really?" I asked. My mom's oncologist was a beautiful black woman. "What's her name?"

"Natasha Jabari." Bebe shrugged as if my question annoyed her.

No one paid any attention to my suddenly burning face, so I didn't have to share that Bebe's mother was my mother's doctor.

My mother has cancer. I caught myself thinking that several times a day, like repetition might help me wrap my brain around it.

When they deemed me presentable, they herded me into the crowded hallways, introducing me to people they liked. A boy I recognized approached.

"Oh God," Brooke whispered. "Oh God. Oh God. Do I look okay?"

I saw frantic desperation cross Brooke's face before I was transfixed by Kevin Sampson's green eyes.

"Hey, Hannah." His voice rumbled under my skin like a cat's purr. Kevin Sampson: tall, tan, so blond his hair was almost white.

Brooke bristled beside me. "Hey, Kevin," she said.

He nodded at her.

Just looking at Kevin made my insides feel like they were falling. You could tell he spent tons of time at the beach—his nose had the cutest pink, peeling spot. His dad was A-list. Definitely A+-list, and had been there lots longer than mine, and Kevin was on the way himself. He'd already been in a Gap commercial and two print ads for Sketchers shoes. He'd had a minor role in a popular but now canceled TV series and had just been cast in his first feature role—in my dad's upcoming movie *Blood Roses*, due to start filming next year.

"Nice to have you here, Hannah," he said. His grin set my face on fire.

When he wandered away from us, Brooke said, "So you know him already?"

I shrugged, as if dismissing it, and said, "He's in my dad's next project."

Brooke stared at me a moment, her expression hungry, then continued with the tour of the school. It consisted of "Here's the library, if you're a dork and actually want to study" and "Here's the computer lab but only losers hang out here." When we walked through an amazingly cool lounge where an enormous climbing wall rose up to high ceilings, Brooke said, "Here's the geek playground. Losers of the world unite here at lunch."

I tried. I made an attempt, even if feeble. I give myself credit for that. "I like to climb," I said. (*Rock climbing* was reason #39.)

"Well, don't do it here," Brooke said. "Not if you want to be anybody."

Be anybody. Did I want to be *anybody?* No, I wanted to be *me.* But did I say anything?

Brooke, Brittany, and Bebe led me through another lounge, outside the cafeteria, where a boy sat playing the piano. His dark, wavy hair hung so far in his eyes I wondered how he could see. He must've been able to though, because he stopped, marked something on the sheet music with a pencil, then continued playing.

"He's still here?" Brooke asked, as if he weren't sitting right there and could hear her. "I didn't think he'd come back this year."

I winced.

"Scholarship," Brooke said. "His parents could never afford to send him here. They work in *craft services*." She said it like providing food on movie sets was the same as begging in the street.

The other girls giggled. I started edging away, willing them to follow. Maybe they'd all laugh and it would turn out to be a joke, like he was their best friend or something.

He gave his head one small shake, tossing the hair out of his eyes, never missing a note of the music. He flicked his eyes at them for a beat, maybe two. His eyes met mine for a split second, stopped—by the fact that he didn't know me maybe—and then returned to the music.

He didn't know me. And this was his chance *to* know me, if I'd *do* something, *say* something, grow a spine, *anything*. But…I didn't.

I didn't say anything in art class, either, when Brooke, Brittany, and Bebe talked and whispered through the whole class, being rude to the teacher who was really cool. I'd read all about him on the school's website and had been psyched to take classes with him.

I loved art, and I did this really cool art at home. It's hard to explain to anyone, but it's one of my favorite things to do: I build cities. Tiny intricate cities out of bits and pieces, trinkets and cool stuff. I told you it was hard to explain, but here, I'll try: Our backyard (surrounded by a privacy fence topped with electric wire) is divided up into garden plots and a tiny pond, all separated by winding stone paths. A couple of the garden plots are devoted to hibiscus and bougainvillea (*orange bougainvillea* is #36) and the Ohio vegetables my mom tries to coax out of the sandy ground, but most of the plots were given over to me to build my miniature cities. The borders of the buildings are decorated with beads, buttons, and gaudy jewelry I get for a quarter at the Salvation Army. (Mom calls me "magpie" because I love the bright shiny pieces best.) The walls are mosaicked with pieces of broken china and pottery. One building has an entire chimney made of snail shells, and another has a barricade fence of starfish. A red toy truck carrying a load of glass Christmas ornaments parks on a boulevard of Scrabble letters. You probably have to see one to really understand it, but just know that when most people see one of my cities, they're blown away. Even adults will crouch down, hug their knees, and stare at it for a long time. My cities are unbelievably cool and complex (if I do say so myself).

My cities make me feel…peaceful, if that's not too dorky. I can make a world where everything is okay, where everything is the way it should be. You can look at it and breathe a sigh of relief.

Those cities are the reason I have things on my list like:

25. Running my hands through a barrel of beads
35. Beach glass
37. Really great thrift stores

(Like once, I found an entire glass jar of buttons at this funky shop in Venice Beach, buttons that looked like typewriter keys, cameo buttons, yellow flower buttons, and tiny copper sun buttons.)

49. Finding surprise stuff inside boxes at yard sales

(One time I found this square, art-deco iridescent peacock broach inside a music box.)

61. Old-fashioned keys (and wondering what they open)

I was actually naïve enough to consider sharing these cities with my new "friends," when Bebe yawned loudly—a fake, mean yawn meant to tell the art teacher how boring he was—and said, "Can you believe we *have* to take this class?"

Brooke rolled her eyes and cracked the enormous wad of purple gum in her jaw.

I didn't tell any of them about the cities.

I still didn't say anything at lunch when they invited me to their table. I gratefully let Brooke lead me, since there's nothing so terrifying as facing a cafeteria alone. Brooke did her hyperventilating "Oh God, oh God" again when Kevin sat down at our table. She had it *bad* for him. He sat across from me and asked how my day had been. I stuttered like a moron. He kept bumping my knees under the table and every time he did, my brain fizzed with white noise for a full thirty seconds.

Brooke held up my baggie of homemade cookies and said, "Oh my God, that's so cute."

I snatched them back and shrugged. "My dad likes to bake."

The girls fell on that like sharks on a bloody limb.

"Ooooh," Brittany squealed, "that's so sweet. Caleb Carlisle bakes cookies."

Kevin laughed. "Caleb Carlisle does it all, man. He's no joke."

I smiled. When he smiled back, I got dizzy.

None of the girls brought their lunches from home. They

paid for intricate, fancy salads, but then picked through them, eating only the lettuce.

The boys ate huge lunches, shoved each other a lot, and talked too loud.

"So, what do you guys do after school?" I asked. "Do you play sports or anything?"

"Tennis," Bebe said. "And it's not too late for us to get you on the team too."

"Actually, I run. I was going to join cross-country this fall and track in the spring."

Brooke grabbed me and put a hand over my mouth. "Never say that out loud ever again!" Brittany and Bebe collapsed in giggles.

I wriggled out from under her grasp, wanting to slug her, but before I could say anything, she said, "Only losers run track, Hannah Anne Carlisle." She said my full name in that mocking singsong. "Don't go hanging out with that geek squad."

I blinked. Was there *anything* about me that was acceptable?

"I have saved you today," Brooke said. "What would you have done without me?"

Maybe been happier, said a little voice in my head. But my own actual voice seemed broken and out-of-order. I stopped eating my sandwich when I noticed all the girls had their giant salads still intact in front of them.

I recognized the piano-playing boy cleaning tables. Brooke followed my gaze and said, "He doesn't pay tuition. He has to do school service."

Kevin bumped his container of ketchup, sending a red dash across the table.

I handed him a napkin but he shrugged. "He'll get it," Kevin said, nodding at the piano-playing boy. "But thanks, Hannah." The way he said my name made me unable to form words.

I'd walked in that morning, a girl who believed she could *Sit with a different group each day at lunch. Make friends with everybody!*

By the time I left that afternoon, I doubted everything about myself.

Chapter 3

66. Finally seeing a trailer for a movie you've been waiting for
67. That screeching sound of packing tape
68. Dogs wearing sweaters
69. Finger painting (especially when you know you're "too old" to be doing it)

I sometimes read the list just to distract myself from the disaster of my life.

87. Wearing a costume
88. The scuttle sound autumn leaves make on the sidewalk
89. Getting yourself all freaked out after a scary movie
90. Warm, fluffy towels straight out of the dryer
91. The skin on top of pudding
92. That smell when the first drops of rain hit concrete
93. Dancing like an idiot when no one is watching

I read the list to distract myself from the fact my mom is dying.

She's so brave battling her cancer that it's not fair at all the cancer is winning. She'd tell me each update—like, "The treatments aren't working"—all matter-of-fact and then say, "But I'm going to keep fighting." Even as Dad started to fall apart in his sorrow, she stayed calm and focused.

94. Cinnamon and sugar on butter-soggy toast
95. Rubbing velvet the wrong way
96. Remembering dreams
97. Playing hooky with Mom

When Mom has really good days, Mom and Dad will let me stay home to be with her. We'll walk on the beach, or watch movies we've already seen but loved, or just sit in the backyard.

Even sick and losing her hair, her beauty seems to light her up from the inside. I feel hideous next to her, all fat, ugly, and cowardly.

I'm such a coward I didn't go out for the cross-country team.

I'm such a coward I didn't join the Art Club.

I'm such a coward I kept sitting with those girls I *know* are horrible. I feel trapped. I don't know how to break free, and each day I don't speak up, it gets harder and harder to figure out how. I'm paralyzed.

Poor Mom. She thought it was *her* fault I've given up everything I love. That hurt worst of all, when she held my hand in the backyard and said, "Hannah Banana, you have to live, sweetie. Have friends. Do the things you want to do. Please, don't stay home because of me. You're so sad and I can't stand that. The best medicine for me is for you to *laugh* and have fun with your friends."

Friends? She wouldn't wish these friends on me if she knew them.

"Are you *sure* you don't want to run cross-country?" she almost begged. "I thought the coach was your favorite teacher."

She is. Mrs. DeTello. She'd been bugging me to join too, but I can't. But I'm *fat*. Poor Mom probably wants me to run because I'm fat.

I miss running. I have dreams about running, but instead of joining cross-country, I at least accepted an invitation to go to the beach with my "new friends" just to make Mom happy. It felt so good to make her happy.

When I said yes to the invite, I didn't know that boys would be there too. My face blazed as I took in Brooke, Brittany, and Bebe in their bikinis. They looked like *models*.

Like *women*. I was the dumpy little girl in a babyish one-piece. A *pink* babyish one-piece, just to make it worse. The boys ignored me, falling all over themselves around the toned bodies of the other girls. I finally waded out into the ocean. The water covered me up; its wildness made me happy.

"Hey, Hannah." Kevin's voice surprised me. He waded out to join me, dragging a surfboard.

"I'm gonna teach you how to surf," he announced.

For a split second, irritation sparked through me. *Teach* me? I already *knew* how to surf. And how about *asking* if I *wanted* to…but the white static his dimples and eyes produced made me mute. I just smiled. What an idiot.

It was fun to be *doing* something, even though I knew Brooke would be jealous. Kevin thought he was an excellent teacher because I picked it up so fast (um, how about *me* being an excellent student?). Time flew and I felt genuinely happy, just the two of us out in the waves.

After a couple good runs in a row, I was just paddling on his board on my stomach and he was treading water near me. He tossed his wet hair out of his eyes, touched my hip, and said, so kindly and sincerely, "You wanna be careful, Hannah. Don't get chubby. You're cute, but you *could* be hot."

I froze, wanting the ocean to swallow me up. I felt *sick*. *He thinks I'm fat.*

Thank God the others shouted at us to come in. Brooke's mom was there to pick us up. Everyone was waiting on me. The hatred and misery shining in Brooke's eyes was sharp enough to cut. My breath dropped funny, and I broke out in a slimy sweat. "I-I have to run to the bathroom," I said, ignoring her mom's impatient sigh. I ran through the hot sand to the stinky beach bathroom, barely making it to a toilet before I vomited. Oh my God. It happened so fast!

Another wave of nausea punched me. I threw up again… and when I stood, the ripple of relief felt…*good*. I splashed water on my face at the sink, rinsed out my mouth, brushed my hair, then headed back to grab my stuff. I felt almost like I floated.

"Sorry," I said, squeezing into the car.

Bebe stared at me, forehead wrinkled.

"What?" I asked.

"You look…I dunno, really good. What did you *do* in there?"

I laughed. *I puked* didn't seem a good answer. I craned my neck to see myself in the rearview mirror: bright eyes, pink cheeks, something…*alive* in me. I felt *happy*.

So happy that later, after dinner, I made myself throw up again just to feel that sensation.

I wrote in my journal, *I think I discovered an amazing secret. When everything is sucky—and when is it not anymore?—this will be my Secret Remedy, my SR.*

I couldn't wait to use it again.

Chapter 4

My purple notebook might say:

77. Root beer floats
78. The smell of crayons
79. Blowing out birthday candles
80. Extra stuff after the credits at the movies
81. Those cool old-fashioned diaries with locks and keys

But my *real* reason to be happy was my secret remedy, my SR. My new best friend.

It was so *easy*.

I used my SR every day.

Mom noticed. It took about three weeks and she said, "You look so pretty." I knew she meant *you've lost weight*. I lied and told her I'd been running. Even my dad said I looked really fit.

It took about four weeks for the kids at school to notice, but when we were at the beach again, I heard Kevin say to Max, "Hannah's got a real body now." Hello. I've *always* had a body. What, was it fake before? You're not a real person until you have a certain kind of body?

That comment would've made the old Hannah mad. But what did I do? I floated on the compliment so much I used my SR twice that day.

When Brooke said, "Maybe you should get a swimsuit that wasn't made for toddlers," I invited the girls to go shopping with me—making my mom happy, going out with friends.

Turns out only Brittany could go. I was actually kind of glad. Brittany was a different person when she wasn't around Brooke. I was sometimes tempted to ask her if she even *liked* Brooke, but that was too dangerous. Anyway, Brittany's eyes got all wide when I tried on an emerald green bikini (crazy expensive for something so tiny) and opened the dressing room door to show her. "You look so totally *hot* in that. You *have* to buy it."

When she said that I turned to look at myself in the mirror. I looked like the other girls at last—no more chubbiness, just curves where they were supposed to be, lean and taut everywhere else. The mirror made me blush.

I had fun hanging out with Brittany, but I was antsy, aware of the clock. The time for my SR approached, and I caught myself anticipating it, *needing* it, growing jittery and nervous until we finally left the mall.

When I got home, I tried to escape to my room, but Mom wanted to see what I'd bought first.

She had a conniption when she saw that bikini. She threatened to take it from me.

"I bought it with my own money!"

"The money is not the point," she said. "This is too adult. It's inappropriate."

"All my friends wear bikinis!" I screamed.

She raised her eyebrows but not her voice. "Hannah. *I* wouldn't wear a bikini this…small, even when I still had a figure." She tried to joke, tried to deflect our argument by poking fun at her poor, pitiful cancer-ravaged body, but I felt like I was possessed. All I could think of was my overdue SR.

I stomped, slammed doors, and hid the bikini deep down in my dresser. I immediately hated myself for it. Mom was sick. Why would I waste a single second shrieking about some stupid scraps of material? I never *wanted* to act like such a brat, but I couldn't stop. When those moods took over, those moods that only started once I'd begun my SR, I'd actually *yearn* to rant and scream. Like all this nasty poison inside of me—this rotten, festering secret—had to find a way out. As I stomped away from my mom that day, I kicked a chair and it hit the door frame where we had glued beach glass into a gorgeous mosaic. Even over my pounding footsteps, I heard the shimmery ping of several pieces falling to the floor.

"Hannah!" she called. "Would you stop? You take everything too far. You need to learn when to quit."

What was she talking about? All I *did* was quit!

I'd quit everything. Running. Art. My cities. Being nice to people. Having a backbone.

The only thing I hadn't quit was the one thing no one else knew I was doing.

Chapter 5

It amazed me how many list items I could recite from memory. Like a whole section of cool Ohio things we don't have in L.A.:

13. The way frosted grass crunches under your feet
14. Big wool sweaters
15. Exploring attics and basements
16. Fang-like icicles that make whole houses look like monster mouths
17. The way a knitted scarf gets crusty with ice when you breathe through it while you're sledding
18. Making snow angels
19. That Styrofoam squeak your shoes make on really cold snow

My brain grabbed for that list like a life raft as I sat in Dr. Jabari's office one night.

My parents and I sat there clutching hands as Dr. Jabari told us the undeniable, irreversible news: my mother was dying.

As Dr. Jabari talked to us, my brain went on overload. I couldn't tell you anything she said about how long we had or what to expect, but I could tell you that she wore emerald earrings, that the polish on two of her nails was chipped, and that her phone hummed seven times while she talked to us, but she didn't show one single sign of hearing it.

Dr. Jabari talked about my mother, but my brain was only capable of grasping the details that wouldn't leave me crumpled on the floor howling at the ceiling. My brain tuned out the doctor's voice and instead registered the orange L.A. sunset through her window, the syrupy lilac scent of her perfume, the photos on her desk.

One photo right in front of me was of Bebe with a boy who must've been her brother.

Her brother clearly had Down Syndrome.

Bebe looked at this boy with what is obviously love. Love you can't fake.

I never said anything to my parents or to Dr. Jabari about knowing her daughter.

I never said anything to Bebe about knowing of her brother.

And I certainly didn't say a word to anyone about the fact that my mother was dying.

Saying it out loud might make it real.

Instead, I focused on my SR.

It made me feel so much better. Like a friend I could always count on.

A friend. That's how pathetic I was. I had an imaginary friend, a friend who tried to convince me that if I were thin enough and pretty enough, Mom couldn't die.

By early October, I used my SR at school for the first time.

By November I used my SR *at least* two times a day. Every day. On Mom's really bad days, it helped me cope.

My poor sick mom, whittled thin by cancer and chemo. My mom, who even then, never complained, but kept living up to her motto, "Pretty is as pretty does," facing each day with her skeletal smile.

I wanted her to see *me* pretty at long last. I wanted her to be able to see me pretty and thin while there was still time.

On Mom's really bad days, I'd just go outside and run and run and run until I couldn't put one foot in front of the other. Twice I ran so far that when I stopped, I was completely lost. That felt good, being lost.

Running like that made me feel crippled the next day. That felt right too, like I deserved the punishment.

The first time I got lost running, I'd come back to myself right next to a little grocery market I didn't recognize. I stood there, clutching my side, panting, and an unbearable, horrific *craving* came over me. *Eat. Eat.* Even as I felt that craving, I felt the deeper craving underneath it taking over me: *use your SR.*

I walked inside that frigid market and bought a pound of jellybeans, two boxes of cherry Pop-Tarts, and two orange Gatorades.

I also put four Little Debbie Oatmeal Creme Pies into the pockets of my running shorts—two in my right pocket, two in my left.

I sat on a bench in a park I didn't know and systematically ate everything I'd just bought and stolen. *Stolen.* I'd never stolen *anything* before. What was happening to me? I was not the kind of person who stole things! But I'd done it without a thought, as naturally as if I did it every day.

When I was finished, I threw it all up into a trash can.

If you think that's bad, just wait. It gets worse.

In December I was caught stealing at school.

A teacher caught me stealing oatmeal cookies from the cafeteria. I thought I was truly busted then, but they didn't get it—not my parents, not my teachers, not the principal. They thought I was on some kind of dare; they didn't really understand why I was taking the food. Why would they? It's not like I was poor and hungry. Almost everyone who goes to my school has parents who make a ton of money, so it had to be a joke, right?

I'd stolen the cookies (and *had* been stealing them for weeks before I was caught) for the same reason I'd stolen food from two other stores since that first market: it took more and *more* food for my SR to work.

I *needed* it to work.

I needed it more than I needed to be a good, honest person who'd never dream of stealing. I'd left that girl behind a long time ago.

I couldn't stand to be in my own skin without the SR.

My parents were *furious* at my stealing and they agreed to the school's punishment for me: I had to spend my lunch hours working in the cafeteria, first helping serve, then cleaning tables. I had to wear a *hair net*. I thought Brooke would disown me then (and I almost wished she *would*), but she, Brittany, and Bebe thought it was cool, like I was some kind of rebel.

You know what was so great about it…well, other than the fact that it became even *easier* to steal food? I didn't have to eat lunch with those girls anymore. Not having to sit with them felt like taking off a heavy backpack after a whole day of hiking. Back in the kitchen, I didn't have to be the Hannah they wanted.

It also meant I couldn't eat with Kevin, though.

The school kitchen was a whole different world. A world I loved. During the actual lunch period while my classmates were out there eating, I was hidden, wearing my plastic apron, hair net, and gloves. There was something so immediate about it, keeping the bins filled as I chopped tomatoes or onions, making sure no one had to stand there and wait too long for what they'd ordered. It gave me that same sense of satisfaction that making my cities used to: I got to see a finished product. I got to see a world functioning with everything in order and control.

That first day I reported to duty, it was the piano-playing scholarship boy who showed me what to do. By then, I knew his name was Jasper.

Jasper Jones. Is that a cool name or what?

I usually only saw him sitting down—at the piano or in class. I knew he was tall because he always looked uncomfortable folded into school furniture, but it startled me to realize I needed to look up at him. He was one of the few people who was taller than me.

From class, I already knew he was smart. *Really* smart. Like a brainiac. But slow. Not slow like mentally slow, but slow in processing. Slow in responding. It took him a while to answer. Brooke would always mutter, "Like maybe this year, moron."

I had noted two things about him: One, he always did his funny head toss to clear the hair out of his eyes before he spoke. And two, he never spoke until he was certain what he was going to say. Like, Brooke, Brittany, and Bebe always did that annoying thing where they shot up their hands first in class, but when the teacher called on them, they'd do that ridiculous, "Well, you know, I, like, I know what the answer is, I just, you know, don't know how to explain it. It's just, like, well, you know (giggle)…um, never mind."

How did the teachers not smack them?

Jasper's hand never shot up. But teachers called on him anyway, especially after two or three other students had flailed around and gotten it wrong. The teacher would turn to Jasper like he was a lifeline. "Jasper? What do you think?"

He was usually right. He always had something interesting to say…it just took him a while to form his thoughts and speak them. The teachers didn't mind waiting for him.

That quality led other kids—well, the mean kids I'd aligned myself with—to mock him as stupid, an idiot. I watched Bebe's face once when Brooke said of Jasper, "What a retard."

I saw the flinch. I flinched too. We made eye contact, but Bebe didn't know I'd seen that picture of her brother. I held that picture in my heart, though, to remember there were complicated sides to everyone. Maybe even Brooke.

I wanted to shrivel up and blow away when I realized Jasper was the person assigned to train me in the kitchen.

"I'm Hannah," I said. I remembered all those horrible times my group had left a revolting mess on the tables. I wanted to add, "I'm sorry."

He looked at me a moment, then smiled. He had a slow smile, like my mom's, only his started in just one corner of his mouth. "I know," he said, with this crooked grin, as if it amused him. "I'm Jasper."

"I know," I said in the same tone he'd used, my old Hannah creeping back for a second.

That made him nod and say, "Well, then, let's see what else you know."

Not much, but I was a quick learner. I surprised myself. It was almost as if when I wasn't around Brooke, Brittany, and Bebe, my brain returned to me. I was always in a white hazy panic when I was around them: what was I going to do wrong, what was I going to say wrong, how was I going to be humiliated, how was Brooke going to punish me for Kevin's attention today? Away from them, I was competent again.

"Hannah kicked butt today," Jasper said later to the kitchen staff. "She's not what we expected."

Had they been talking about me? I felt my face burn.

When the adult staff had all gone back to their work and weren't paying any attention anymore, I whispered, "I'm sorry. I know what you think. But-but I'm not like that."

He'd taken off the bandana he wore in the kitchen, so his hair hung in his eyes again. He tossed his head, then tilted it. His eyes were the color of iced tea. Up close I saw that one iris had a triangle of gold in it, like a slice of pie had been taken, revealing the yellow dish beneath. "You know what I think," he repeated. I couldn't read his meaning.

"What did you expect?" I asked.

He blinked. "When people have to work back here as punishment, it usually turns out to be punishment for us. But you were good."

"Oh." How stupid was I, thinking that anyone paid attention to me or my mean friends?

He kept gazing down at me, his face open. "You're not like what?"

I tried to will the red to stay out of my face. "You know, like"—I tilted my head out toward the tables—"those girls I sit with at lunch. I'm-I'm not like them."

He gazed at me a minute. "The B-Squad?" he asked.

"B-Squad?" I thought he meant *bee* squad, which really made perfect sense. All that venom.

"Yup," he said, and turned away from me, back to work. He was unloading a cart of stuff that had just been delivered at the back door onto the pantry shelves, even though the head woman, Pam, had told us we could go.

"Why do you call them that?" I asked.

"One guess." He picked up the biggest can of green beans I'd ever seen and hefted it onto the shelf.

"Because we're...bitches?"

He stopped, tossed his hair out of his eyes, and gazed at me again. Then his lopsided smile emerged and he *laughed*. "Ha! Sure, that works too!" He returned to the cans.

"Why, then?"

"Because their names all start with B and I can't tell them apart. They look the same, they dress the same, they talk the same, they think the same."

I caught myself grinning, even though technically, this criticism applied to me as well. "They don't look the same," I chided him, but teasing. "Bebe is..."

He stopped again, the top shelf of his cart empty. "Bebe is what?"

"You know."

He tilted his head. "She's what?" I caught a little edge in his voice. He was so hard to read!

"She's black!" I said. "So you can tell *her* apart. I mean they don't *look* the same."

He waved his hand, as if brushing away a pesky fly. "I didn't mean anything that *surface*. I can't see past the stuff on the inside. There's not one individual thought between them."

Wow. "I-I thought everyone—You don't think they're pretty? Bebe's the prettiest."

He snorted. "Pretty is as pretty does."

I gasped. "My mom says that all the time."

He studied me. "Your mom is Annabeth Anderson?"

I nodded, then braced for it.

"Your mom is one smart woman."

Not "beautiful" not "gorgeous" not "hot." Not the crude things I'd overhead Max say.

Smart.

I stood there, wondering how to end this conversation and get Jasper out of the cafeteria. I couldn't leave first because I still had a mission there in the kitchen.

He'd almost finished unloading the cart. "So why'd you say 'we,'" he asked, "even though you said you weren't like them?"

Before I could answer, Pam came out from the main kitchen. "Jasper! What are you still doing back here? Go play!"

Go play? What, was he some kind of child?

He laughed and said, "I'm going! I'm going!" and pushed the now empty cart back to the door. Then he went, without another glance at me, tossing his plastic apron in the trash as he walked out the wide swinging doors. Pam didn't notice me either; she turned around and walked back into the kitchen.

My heart pounded in my ears. *Perfect.* It was perfect. Could I pull it off?

Ten minutes later, I slipped out those doors and through the empty cafeteria to the bathrooms.

Piano music trailed me. That's what Pam had meant by "Go play."

I glanced up at the clock. I had five minutes until class started. I'd be late, but it was worth it.

Chapter 6

51. Sleeping in on rainy mornings
52. Real whipping cream
53. Silly Putty
54. Slinkies
55. Hammocks

I sometimes had to repeat sections of my list just to get through the morning classes to lunch.

I lived for lunch and my kitchen job. Okay, I admit, mostly because I could keep stealing food, but also because it was one of the few places I felt like a real person. I could breathe, be competent, and think my own thoughts. I got good at noticing what needed to be done and taking care of it without asking. Nobody ever gave me the cold shoulder for what landed me there in the first place. They were all nice to me. To *me*. Not because of who my parents were.

It became important to me to prove to Jasper that I wasn't like the rest of the B-Squad.

My status within the group had clearly changed. I didn't belong to the Squad, but they wouldn't truly release me to belong to anyone else either. Brooke hated me, and that meant Brittany and Bebe were required to as well, but Brooke couldn't write me off the way she truly wanted to because of Kevin—the way Kevin sought me out, touched the back of my neck, and said, "Hannah's cool" all forced Brooke to tolerate me. Plus, there was now the connection between Kevin and my dad, who were filming *Blood Roses* together, and Brooke was obsessed with my dad. She worshipped Dad in spite of me.

Brittany has this picture of Dad, shirtless, hanging in her locker, this picture that was in *Entertainment Weekly*. Bebe said Dad was "totally hot," which is gross to say in front of me, but not as gross as what Brooke said. Right in front of me she said, "I'd marry him."

Eww. That's so wrong on *so* many levels.

Just like the rest of my life.

My SR has stopped working. I've gained weight. I have this giant, swollen, moon face with bloodshot eyes all bruised purple underneath. My teeth are stained gray, no matter how many Crest Whitening Strips I use.

The school counselor pulled me out of class for a talk. My pulse hammered in my ears as I walked to her office on legs filled with ice water. This was it. I was busted. I looked at the bright orange lockers, the green-and-white tiled floor, and thought *nothing will ever be the same. Everything is about to change. My life is over.*

I trembled by the time I took a seat in her office. I tucked my hands under my thighs.

When she said, "Hannah, many of your teachers are concerned about you," I wanted to throw myself to the floor, hug her legs, and beg, "Please! You can't make me stop! I'll die without it!"

She leaned toward me, elbows on her knees (I could see her pink lace bra), her forehead all wrinkled. "Hannah, are you using drugs?"

What? My spine stiffened. Images of my dad's mug shot flashed through my mind. "Are-are you asking that because of my dad's past problems?" I made my voice as snotty and offended as I could muster through my surprise.

"No, we're asking this because of your perpetually bloodshot eyes, your frequent nosebleeds, and your calm, high appearance when you arrive late every day to your after-lunch class."

Wow.

She thought I was "self-medicating" my grief over my mother's cancer. I expected euphoria that they were so off base, but a crushing blanket of defeat settled on me, a blanket so heavy it felt like that awful lead thing the dentist drapes on you to take X-rays of your teeth. Part of me wanted them to know the truth and, more importantly, to *make me stop it.*

That surprised me, the realization that I *wanted* to stop it.

I denied everything. She didn't believe me. I walked back to class, and the orange lockers and the green-and-white tile mocked me. *Nothing* had changed. I was trapped.

So, this conversation with the counselor only accomplished the double anxiety of knowing I was still on my own in this, but that people were paying attention to me. I didn't want anyone paying attention to me.

Unfortunately, the attention kept coming.

In art class, we'd been assigned to do life-size portraits of people cut out of thin wood.

Most people had chosen to paint themselves.

I had chosen to paint my mother.

Kevin chose to paint me.

Okay, okay, I admit when Kevin announced me as his subject, my heart raced. My stomach somersaulted. I thought

I might have an asthma attack (and I don't have asthma). Of all the people he could've chosen, he chose *me*.

"Ooh," Brittany whispered. "I think he likes you."

The thought made me dizzy.

I saw the tears in Brooke's eyes before she cut class.

After a couple days of work, though, it became obvious that Jasper was painting me too. My stomach felt like it held a brick. Why was he doing this to me? I thought we were friends!

"Well, well, well," Brooke said, "aren't you just Little Miss Popular?"

"Ooh," Bebe said, loud enough for him to hear, "maybe Jasper likes you too."

The girls and Kevin all snickered as if they'd suggested some hideous mutant liked me.

What could I say? It was an impossible situation, a minute that lasted a hundred years. The B-Squad expected me to react, to snicker also or shriek "Eww!"

I looked at Jasper, whose head was bent over his painting, his hair in his eyes. He didn't look at us, but I knew he was listening, waiting. *Why?* Why did he have to go and put us both in this position? Who asked him to paint me anyway?

There was no way to win. I just made a face at the girls, hoping I could convey to them my "whatever" sentiment without Jasper seeing it. But that wasn't enough. "Oooh," Brooke sang, "maybe Hannah likes him back!"

Kevin looked at me, curious. *Why?* Why was this happening?

"You've got competition, Kevin." Brooke sneered.

Were my chances to be normal, to be liked, being ruined just because some strange boy had decided to draw me? How was this *my fault?*

Kevin asked, "Do you like him?"

My face *hurt* with heat. "No!" I whispered, the word a rasp that skinned my throat.

Fortunately, Jasper walked away to wash out his brushes in the sink. His back was to us and the water made a good masking noise.

The girls collapsed in giggles. Bebe mimed puking.

Kevin winked at me. "You're my Mona Lisa," he said. I floated for a moment, until Brooke's wounded, hateful eyes burst my bubble, and Jasper's back—spending far too long at the sink—made my throat ache.

"I didn't mean to make you uncomfortable yesterday in art," Jasper said the next day while we shredded lettuce in the cafeteria kitchen.

I shrugged, hating *and* loving that he'd brought it up. I'd felt clumsy and pained, bumping around the incident without speaking of it. I couldn't believe *he* was apologizing to *me*.

"That was awkward," Jasper said.

I nodded. "I just—I wish you'd told me," I said.

He paused, his gloved hands on the lettuce.

"I would've told you not to pick me," I said. "They're just going to be mean to you about it."

He put his lettuce down and turned to face me. He tossed his hair out of his eyes and looked at my face like I'd written something there. He took his time to form his thoughts, like usual. While he did, it struck me that the golden triangle in the iris of his eye would be a pretty cool detail to capture in a painting.

"I wanted to paint you. They don't have the power to stop me from doing what I want."

The simplicity of those words filled me with awe. And sorrow.

And shame.

"So, *do* you like Kevin?" he asked. His face was hard to read, but I thought I saw genuine curiosity and maybe a little bewilderment.

"I just—I don't know. He—he's okay." I sounded like a moron, but knew my hot, blazing face gave Jasper his answer.

He nodded once, as if checking in with himself that he'd said what he needed, then he returned to the lettuce.

Three Bad Things happened, almost in a row, after the New Year.

First, Brooke invited me to her pool party.

I was relieved and terrified to get the invitation. I might've made up some excuse not to go, but one day when my mom felt good enough to pick me up from school, Brooke had yelled, "See you at the party, Hannah Anne Carlisle!"

"What party?" my mom had asked, glowing with joy like *she'd* been invited. It struck me: Mom worried that I was a dork and had no friends. I told her I didn't really want to go, but she was so *into* it. I wanted so much to make her happy. I was trying so hard to lose weight so she could see me beautiful just once. So I could be "pretty is as pretty does." I knew I was neither, but I wanted to be at least one for her. She wanted me to go to the party. So I went.

I pulled that green bikini out of the drawer where I'd stuffed it the day I bought it.

The thing was, Mom was *right* about the bikini. I wore it, but then felt so uncomfortable, like I was on display. I *thought* I wanted the boys to look at me like they looked at Brooke, but when they did, I hated it.

From the moment I arrived, I only wanted to be home.

Bebe made fun of me for going off the diving board and actually swimming. Hello, wasn't this a *pool* party? I longed to honestly *swim*, just like I longed to run. I'd started having dreams about running. In the dreams, I was tiny and ran in one of my own miniature cities where everything was tidy and perfect. Mom had asked about my cities recently, and in an attempt to do *something* she could admire, I'd started making a new one. I was halfway finished. I wished I was home doing that, instead of in Brooke's swimming pool.

At least in the water I was sort of hidden, instead of posing around the edges trying to suck in my belly and keep my arms crossed over my chest. In the deeper end, where it was dark and out of the lights, Kevin swam over to me and said, "Who's that beautiful mermaid I see?" He was *so cute* he made my brain go to mush. The word *beautiful* turned me into an idiot. I grinned at him, so grateful. I held on to the side of the pool under the diving board, and he swam up right beside me. Our bare shoulders touched, sending a shudder all through me.

But then, I could hardly believe what happened next. I

know, I know, what a cliché, right? But I *mean* it. I literally could not believe it was happening. Under the water, where no one else could see, Kevin grabbed my butt! When I shoved his hand away, he laughed and tried to put his hand on my *chest*.

I froze, the white noise in my head so loud. For a split second I actually thought *Is this what I'm supposed to do? Am I supposed to let him?*

I saw Max squinting through the dark at us. I pushed Kevin hard. "What are you doing?" I whispered.

"What do you *think* I'm doing, you moron?"

Nice. *You moron?* Yeah, like that was really going to convince me to let him!

He swam back to me again with his hands out, chuckling, so I splashed him in the face then climbed out of the pool.

Oh my God! He'd never even kissed me! I couldn't believe he did that right there in the pool with everyone about twenty yards away from us. I wrapped myself in my towel and stood near the other girls, but Brooke sneered, "Have fun in there?"

By this point the boys were gathered in a circle in the pool whispering and snickering. I hated them all. I just wanted to leave. All of a sudden, it hit me: the idea that I could use my SR right there to feel better. If only I could feel good and relaxed, then I'd be able to sit there like the other girls and have fun.

Here's the thing: once I *thought* about my SR, it took hold of me. There was no turning back. I was going to do it.

There wasn't much to eat out by the pool, just some chips and pretzels. I took my gym bag into the house and took everything I could find in the cupboards. I found good pasta salad in the fridge. Brooke's mom almost caught me, but I put the Tupperware container into my bag just in time. She was all paranoid about why I was in the house. I think she thought I was going to steal something, since everybody knew I got caught stealing at school. It struck me that she was *right*. I'd turned into a thief and a liar. Everything felt so out of control. I told her I had to use the bathroom, dashed in there, and turned the fan on high. I didn't think I could do it—with her knocking on the door, I couldn't eat very much. I only had a few handfuls of the pasta salad. The SR felt totally different. It was harder, and I saw lots of white sparkling lights and my fingers swelled up.

Brooke's mom wouldn't stop knocking on the door being all nosy. When I opened the door and told her I felt sick to my stomach, she gave me 7-UP and some lip gloss. *Lip gloss?*

I thought Jasper would like that detail—giving lip gloss

to someone who was nauseated. But then, I'd have to tell him the whole story. Starting with a party he wasn't invited to.

When I went back outside, I caught a glimpse of Brooke and Kevin *making out* under the diving board!

As I waited for my heart to unclutch, Bebe sidled up next to me and said, "Well. Finally. Maybe he'll get over his obsession with you and they can get back together."

I swallowed. *Back* together?

I went home and cut my green bikini into tiny pieces with a pair of scissors.

I wrote in my journal, *The SR isn't working. My throat hurts all the time. I'm still fat. It isn't fair. I can't stop, though. I can't sleep without it. I need something good. My life sucks.*

Aunt Izzy came to visit from Ohio, to spend time with my mom. She would've been here lots earlier, but she'd been in Ghana, in West Africa, working on her newest documentary about African orphans.

Aunt Izzy walked into baggage claim and narrowed her eyes at me. She put her hands on my face and rubbed her thumbs over my chubby cheeks, then under my eyes, where broken blood vessels mottled purple. She took both my hands in hers, turning mine palm down as if searching for something, then stopped, with her thumbs on the middle knuckles of my right hand.

Standing right there at baggage claim, before she'd even really said hi to any of us, she turned to my mom and said, "Why didn't you tell me Hannah was bulimic?"

I about fainted.

The thing was, my mom hadn't told her because my parents didn't *know*.

Dad was talking to some fans and missed that little blurt.

Aunt Izzy used to be anorexic. Like really, truly anorexic. She had to be in the hospital for *six months* when she was in high school. My mom said Izzy had nearly died.

So, Aunt Izzy knew a little bit about eating disorders and she was on to me like *that*.

That night, while Dad was on set, Aunt Izzy had a long talk with Mom about it. I know because I eavesdropped on them, terrified. Aunt Izzy convinced Mom to take me to a counselor.

I hardly slept that night.

The next morning, though, Mom was really sick and the appointment never got scheduled.

By Sunday evening, Mom had to go back to the hospital, and my SR got shoved deep down in the trash can, like all the wrappers from my binges.

I felt so guilty. I pleaded with the universe, I pleaded with God—*I'll go to a therapist every single day if you just let her live!*

Monday at school, as I worked in the cafeteria, Jasper asked, "So, how was that pool party?"

My stupid face scalded red again. How did he even know about it?

"Sucked." I hoped he wouldn't see my face. No such luck.

He tilted his head. "You okay?"

I nodded, then reached up to pat my flaming cheeks. I saw his eyes follow my hands.

"What's that mark on your fingers?" he asked.

I froze. He took my right hand, and it gave me a shudder— but a much better shudder than when my bare shoulder had touched Kevin's. He held my hand in both of his, gently— like my hand was a baby bird—and turned it palm down. He rubbed his thumbs over the red mark across my middle knuckles, just like Aunt Izzy had. "What *is* that?" he asked, his voice full of concern that confused me.

I became acutely aware of the laughter from out in the cafeteria, the thumping of my own heart, the musky-under-the-clean-soapy-smell of Jasper's body.

I pulled my hand away, my heart zipping like I was afraid. *Afraid of what?* "I don't know," I said. "A blister I guess."

He tilted his head, that golden wedge in his eye flashing at me. "Who gets blisters on their knuckles?" he asked in a serious tone, like he was trying to solve a mystery.

I shrugged again. I think the mark was from my teeth. But I couldn't tell him that.

He nodded and returned to the lettuce.

I remembered that day in art class and wished I could replay the scene. I longed for another take. If I could have it, I'd play it totally differently.

The second Bad Thing happened the week after the pool party when it was time to hang up the life-size portraits.

Kevin's reaction to me after the party confused me. I thought he'd be mean to me, but he was overly friendly, winking at me, calling out "Hey, Hannah" whenever he saw me. This always prompted the boys with him to snicker. Then, he'd turn and make out with Brooke!

I also thought the B-Squad would be done with me. But

it was like they kept me around to be the permanent whipping boy or insulting girl or whatever you wanted to call me. They were openly disdainful; at least, Brooke and Bebe were, saying things like, "Don't you know not to hook up with a boy on the first date?"

"I *didn't!*"

They snorted. Brooke pursed her lips and raised her waxed eyebrows. "Not what *I* heard."

Great. I *hadn't* let Kevin grope me, but he'd told everyone we'd done it? And how pathetic was that, Brooke throwing herself all over a boy who said he'd been after someone else?

I prayed word of his daughter's "hooking up" wouldn't somehow reach my dad on the set. I hated when Kevin was at school with his creepy winks and pats on my shoulder, but I hated it equally when he was absent because I knew he was with my dad. I made myself sick imagining worst-case scenarios of what he might say about me.

I was terrified Kevin was going to do something hideous to his portrait of me, like give me zits or make me really fat, but he didn't. His portrait was way more beautiful than the real me. I couldn't look at it without blushing.

Jasper's, though, looked like *me*. It freaked me out a little; it was so accurate it was like a photo. He even got details like the fact that one of my eyebrows was higher than the other. That my cheeks were all chubby.

He even included that mark on my knuckles.

I volunteered to help the art teacher hang the portraits because I wanted to be sure to hide the portraits of me. Mr. G. and I lined the front entry hall and the two side halls with them. They looked like real people at first glance. I hung up Kevin's portrait of me on a patch of wall behind the counselor's room; during the day, when her door was open, no one would see the portrait.

As Mr. G. and I worked our way into the front hall, I heard Kevin's voice around the corner back by the counselor's office. He was talking to Brooke and Bebe and Max. I heard Brooke say my name.

"That's pretty damn good, Kevin," Max said.

"*Too* good, if you know what I mean," Brooke said.

"Yeah, you did cheat a little!" Bebe's laugh echoed down the hall. Panic built inside me, making it hard to breathe.

Kevin laughed and said, "Well, I couldn't exactly put her fat butt on my final project."

They all *laughed*. I heard Brooke's distinctive laugh; she sounded like a hyena.

"I thought you *liked* her butt," Brooke jeered.

"Please," Kevin said, "what was I supposed to do? She *threw* that butt at me."

I dropped my hammer and fled. I couldn't let them know I'd heard them.

Those first two Bad Things kind of seem like nothing compared to the third.

The third Bad Thing was my mom died.

Chapter 1

There's like a whole month of my life I don't remember.

We knew it was coming. We knew she was going to die...
but there's no way, no matter how much warning you get, to
be ready. There's no way to avoid being ripped open, crushed
until there is nothing left of you.

My dad and I pretty much fell apart.

Everyone says that, *fell apart*, but it's what it truly felt
like—like actual pieces of us fell away, scattering around,
until there were *too many* fragments to possibly repair.
How could you even *begin* to fix us? The idea was too
overwhelming—easier to ignore the shards, to just get used
to being broken.

I miss her. It seems so stupid to even say that. It's such an
understatement. I *miss* her. I look for her and she's not there.

After she died, Dad started drinking. Too much. I pre-
tended not to notice.

After she died, I wrote a whole section of "Mom things" on my list:

102. The way Mom gave me butterfly kisses with her eyelashes when I was little
103. That lemon meringue lotion she used, so she always smelled like dessert
104. The way she called me beautiful

"Hey, beautiful, what are you thinking?" she'd ask, coming out to the backyard where I crouched working on my cities

105. The way she'd actually listen
106. Mom's smile when I walked into the room
107. The way she called me Hannah Banana
108. The look on her face the times I watched her studying my cities when she didn't know I was looking
109. Our beach glass door frame in moonlight
110. Mom's dorky birthday poems
111. The way Mom sang off-key to the car radio

If she were still here, I wouldn't be such a disaster.

Sometimes I sit and picture her, the way she'd hardly ever wear makeup when she wasn't on a set, and she looked so clean. Or I remember being in the ocean, seeing how long I could hold my breath and float underwater—the way she yanked me up by the hair, her face panicked, thinking I'd drowned. Her fear—which showed she loved me—felt like a solid thing in the air around us. Then she laughed, choked, and said, "Hannah! You always take things too far."

She was right.

She was so, so right. I'd taken my SR too far. No longer my friend, but a creepy stalker I couldn't get rid of. It scared me and I wanted to stop it more than anything in the world.

No, that's not true.

More than anything in the world, I wanted my mom back.

But stopping the SR? That was second.

Chapter 8

My newest reason to be happy should've been to *have* a reason to be happy again! I hadn't been able to up come with anything except stuff that had to do with my mother since she died, but now I had a new one: *blue icing*. I could finally add a #114 to my list:

112. The way Mom always smiled and never rushed her fans when they approached her
113. Dreams where my mom is still alive and healthy
114. BLUE ICING!

This blue icing was the best thing to happen to me all that day. No, all that week. Maybe the entire two weeks I'd missed school after Mom died. That's all I could think about when I got back in the car with my pissed-off dad: that bright blue icing on the cupcakes would be *perfect*.

My brain stuck on that blue icing even though my dad had just caught me shoplifting. I didn't steal the cupcakes. Please. Where was I supposed to hide a plastic container of four cupcakes? I'm not *that* fat. Dad caught me slipping a Three Musketeers bar into the pocket of my cargo pants.

This floating feeling washed over me: *Maybe this is it. I'm busted. It's over. I don't want to be this person. I* know *stealing is wrong.* The floating kind of felt like relief. But mostly it felt like a freak-out. I really needed it that night.

He caught me. I still couldn't believe it. Most of the time he was so clueless. Mom had been too. Maybe she never noticed me stealing because she usually felt so awful it took all her energy just to stay upright and walk through the grocery store. But Dad didn't have that excuse. (At least when he was sober, which he *seemed* to be right now. Who knew anymore?) Didn't he ever wonder why I always waited in the car when he went in that one market in Malibu? One of the cashiers there had caught me stealing a loaf of bread.

I had to give up a lot of the food I'd swiped when Dad caught me…but not all of it. I still had the most important stuff. I just hoped Dad couldn't hear the crinkling noise of the plastic baloney wrapper I'd shoved down the front of my pants. The baloney was so cold it almost burned. I'd lifted it from the fridge near the deli counter.

Little bulges poked out of Dad's tight jaw, his knuckles white on the steering wheel. I wished I could tell him I was sorry. I wished I could do better. I wished I could just tell him the truth, so he would save the day and make everything okay like he did in his movies.

I wondered if he hated me. For being alive. When Mom is dead.

I wished he would talk or say something, even if he yelled at me.

Somewhere down beneath the lunch meat in my pants, the candy bar started to melt. Another Three Musketeers, soft and mushy. I hated how the candy bar felt, pressing against me, like gross Kevin's hands in the pool. Just thinking of him brought back that prickling, frozen shock. Gross stupid moron. Now they all acted like idiots around me, snickering and stuff. I hated them. I hated that whole school. My classes, the teachers, everyone.

That's not true. I didn't hate DeTello. I think she suspected something. I didn't think she suspected the SR, but she kept writing these notes on my assignments and keeping me after class to tell me I have power and potential and I can do anything.

I don't think she *meant* to lie, but I didn't feel it. I looked inside and I didn't see it. I remembered that I *used* to see it.

I didn't know what happened. I couldn't remember when I started impersonating Hannah Carlisle instead of actually being her.

In the car, my dad still didn't talk.

Why couldn't everything be the way it used to be, before I started this disgusting habit, with my mom alive and my dad not hiding bottles of Scotch all over the house? I clutched the cupcakes. Thank God for the blue icing.

We took the groceries into the house in silence. Maybe Dad wouldn't talk to me ever again. Mom and Dad's best friends, Sean and Laila—both actors too—were coming over for dinner. *That could work in my favor. Maybe that will keep Dad too occupied to deal with me.*

I reached into a bag, pulled out the tabloid I'd bought, and used it to mask the bag of Ho Hos. Maybe if I was just really casual…

"Hannah," Dad said, "we need to talk about what happened."

I let the Ho Hos drop back into the bag, but kept the magazine.

"Why did you shoplift?" he asked.

"I *didn't* shoplift."

"You were *going* to shoplift. You just got caught."

"I was going to put them back."

I wished Dad could see himself, his eyes popping out of his head. He opened his mouth and held out his hands like he was totally ready to freak. Looking at him right then, it was hard to believe he was actually a pretty good actor. But I felt bad for him. You'd think if your wife just died, you'd be too distracted to flip about something like this.

All I wanted was to get rid of the candy bar and baloney. I had to get to my room.

"I'm sorry, but I don't believe that," Dad said. "You're lucky *I* caught you. If someone else had seen you, they would've pressed charges. It would've been all over the tabloids. And I'm standing here thinking that maybe I *should've* gotten the manager."

Sweat trickled between my belly and the lunch meat. I knew he meant it. I knew it in the store; that's why I gave up the candy bar, the Peppermint Patty, and the two Oatmeal Cream Pies. When my dad was mad, he didn't say stuff he didn't mean, like some people. When Dad was mad, he *only* told the truth (well, except about his own secret remedy, that is).

"You want to get arrested?" he asked. "You want to have a criminal record?"

Like you? I wanted to snap, but didn't. The vein in his forehead turned purple.

"You stole from school, and I caught you today. Are there more times we don't know about?"

You have no idea. My hot skin itched. I wished I could unzip it and peel it off.

He yelled and made me jump. "Damn it, Hannah! I don't need this crap right now!"

I'd never seen him look like that before—a hot red spot shone from both cheeks. His eyes glittered like those crazy street people who act like they want to fight you.

Was he calling *me* crap? He didn't need crappy old me anymore?

I surprised myself by screaming back, "Well, I don't need *you* anymore either!" Screaming felt really good, even though my throat was raw.

His face shifted again and I felt like I was watching him on film. His eyes welled up with tears and everything about him softened.

"No, no, no, Hannah, that's not what I meant." He reached for me, to hug me, but I backed away. "Don't *ever* think that. I *do* need *you*. I didn't mean I don't need you, I just…I don't understand this. Why are you doing this?"

I was glad he said he needed me, but I had everything ready upstairs in my room. I needed to get the candy bar out of my crotch. I needed to *start* or I would go crazy.

70

Dad whispered, "I'm sorry."

I nodded. "It's okay." Perfect exit line. I picked up the magazine and cupcakes again. Forget the Ho Hos. I'd get them later. I started to leave the room.

"Whoa. Excuse me. Where do you think you're going? We have groceries to unload and dinner to make." He paused, all dramatic. "And I want you to talk to me about the shoplifting."

Oh my God! I slammed the magazine down and longed to smash my fist into the cupcake container lid. I yanked one of the reusable cloth bags toward me. I shoved stuff into a pantry cupboard. I slammed cans and each bang fueled me more. I couldn't help myself. The SR was taking over. It was beginning and I wanted to go give in to it. Dad was ruining everything. I flung the cupboard shut so hard it bounced back open.

Dad started unloading groceries too, and that meant he wasn't watching my every move. Maybe I could snag the bag with the Ho Hos.

"You want candy bars?" he said. "You can buy candy bars. *I'll* buy you candy bars."

He stopped unloading groceries and touched my shoulder. I jerked away. I didn't even mean to, but I couldn't *stand* to be touched, not when it was beginning. This was turning into an emergency.

"What is this *really* about?" he asked.

How could he be so stupid? Did he really not get it? Dad turned to reach into the bag I'd left unguarded. I wanted to tackle him when he pulled out the bag of Ho Hos.

"Hannah! Did you put this in the cart?" He shook his head and said, "A dozen Ho Hos?" like it was a bag of human hands or something. He dropped the bag and snatched up the receipt. "These better be paid for, or I swear to God, we're getting back in the car this second."

Where did he think I could hide a bag of twelve Ho Hos? Was he insane?

"You're in luck," he said, sticking the receipt in his pocket. "But you'll be paying me back for these."

"Why? I can't have a snack because you're spending too much money on booze?" Saying that felt as good as slamming a door.

Dad's hand twitched and I thought he might slap me. I sort of wished he would.

He tossed the bag to me, but I didn't catch it. It hit me in the chest and fell to the floor. When I bent to get it, the baloney packet dug into my gut. Something hot and burning rolled up my throat. I swallowed hard. I stood up with the bag, dizzy.

Suddenly I didn't *want* to leave the room. If I left, I knew what I'd do. Maybe Dad would make me help with dinner or something. This dinner was kind of a big deal, after all—our first guests since Mom died…even though Sean and Laila hardly counted as guests. Maybe if I stayed here in the kitchen, the feeling would go away.

"The money is hardly the point," Dad said. But he didn't tell me what the point *was*. Why couldn't he see what was happening to me? Why couldn't Izzy have told *him* instead of Mom?

I stood there in our kitchen, holding the bag of Ho Hos against my chest like a pillow while Dad started fixing dinner. I wanted him to talk about it. I *wanted* to stop it, I really did.

I sat down at the kitchen island and tore open the bag. Inside were six packages of two Ho Hos each. I took one out. Dad was doing something at the stove, but he glanced at me over his shoulder. I could tell he was disgusted, but he tried to hide it. I shoved in a big mouthful, eating half the Ho Ho in one bite. Dad's lips curled down. I ate the other half. When I licked the cream off my fingers, he turned away. Without looking at me, he laid four chicken breasts on the grill, and said, "If you're going to eat high fat, you might as well eat *better tasting* fat. I mean, that cream filling tastes like Styrofoam and the icing has no flavor."

Icing! I remembered the cupcakes. I needed to eat that blue

icing. I'd already had one Ho Ho, so I'd be sure to go way past the blue icing when it reappeared. Just to make sure.

I picked up a cupcake and licked the icing off the top. Dad pinched up his face and turned away. I got every bit of icing I could, then I ate the cupcake. If I wasn't safe from the SR sitting in the same room with him, then I knew it was up to me to protect myself. The blue icing was all I had.

I could tell from the ingredients that Dad was making Thai salad with grilled chicken, my very favorite. He cut a lime in half. When I opened a second pack of Ho Hos, he glanced at me, his face and neck all red. He ground the lime against the juicer.

I pulled the magazine back out of the grocery bag with chocolatey fingers. I'd put it in the cart along with the Ho Hos because Dad's picture was on the cover—not the feature, not this time (Sean and Laila were, though), but one of the smaller boxes. Mom never wanted me to read stuff about Dad or our family before she read it first, but she wasn't here anymore to stop me.

Dad chopped vegetables, whacking that knife around, making more noise than he needed to. He'd probably cut off a finger and blame it on me. I flipped through the magazine.

I found the article. The first picture was a full page of Dad on the set of *Blood Roses*. Production had been halted for nearly a month because of…because of Mom. He'd just gone back to it two days ago. The photo was good, except that Kevin was in the background.

I ate another Ho Ho.

"Hannah," Dad said, his voice all shocked like I'd picked my nose in public or something.

I ignored him.

He reached out and moved the bag of Ho Hos away from me. We glared at each other.

I kept reading the article. *Blood Roses* was about vampires. My dad was playing a vampire. He had to ride a horse English style and wear period costumes. It was set in the 1890s.

"I thought this was a serious film," Aunt Izzy had said when she heard it was about vampires.

"It is," Mom said, sounding like she was defending Dad.

Mom had been lying in bed, and Aunt Izzy was painting Mom's toenails bright scarlet. Izzy started telling stories from when she and Mom were kids. My grandparents had passed away when I was really little, so I loved those stories about Mom's childhood, because there weren't many sources for me to get them from, and I was hungry for every single detail about my mother I could get. I think that's the day it finally hit me that I was going to lose her, that she really, truly was going to die and I wouldn't have her anymore. As Aunt Izzy and Mom told stories, I sat cross-legged on the floor in the bedroom, trying to soak up every word.

"I've always loved vampires," Mom said. I'd never known that. I loved vampires too. "When I was young," she said, "I wanted to *be* a vampire." She turned her bald head to me and smiled. "I read *Dracula* and *Salem's Lot*. I read every book and story I could find with vampires in it. I used to leave my window open at night, and I'd take out the screen, hoping a vampire would come in my window and make me a vampire too."

"No vampires ever came," Aunt Izzy said, her nose close to Mom's toes. "But one night a possum came in through that window and your grandma was pretty darn mad at your mom."

I giggled. "What happened?"

Aunt Izzy grinned as she kept polishing. "This possum was sitting on the couch, hissing at everyone in the morning. All three of our worthless dogs were cowering by the front door."

"How'd you get it out?"

"Your grandma chased it off, whacking it with a broom," Aunt Izzy said, laughing. "And after that, she'd check your mom's windows every night."

"Why did you want to be a vampire?" I asked her.

Aunt Izzy lifted her head from Mom's toes. "You are amazing," she said to me. "Do you know I never once asked that question? Even after the possum. I never stopped to ask *why*."

"Hmm," my mom murmured. She ran a hand over her patchy head, tucking her nonexistent hair behind her ear. "I wanted to live forever," she whispered.

I stopped breathing. Her words ached inside me like I'd pressed on a bruise.

"There are so many things I want to do and see, and even back then I worried I'd run out of time," Mom said. "If I were immortal, I'd have forever to explore and try everything I wanted."

I'd fought really hard not to cry.

Aunt Izzy had cried, though, her tears dripping down onto Mom's new red toenails.

"You certainly didn't want to live forever," Mom said, in a joking tone, trying to make Aunt Izzy laugh. "There I was, trying to attain immortal life, and you seemed determined to speed yours to a hasty end."

Aunt Izzy smiled, kind of sad. "I know," she said. "I'm sorry."

Mom lifted a foot and tried to wipe a tear that hung from the corner of Aunt Izzy's mouth with her toe. Her polish wasn't dry, though, and she'd left a red streak, like blood.

I thought about that conversation now. No way did I want to live forever. I didn't even want to live *right now*. It would be cool to be a vampire, though, because if your life sucked as bad as mine did (ha ha, no pun intended), you could just walk out to meet the sunshine and end it all.

I pulled the bag of Ho Hos back to me.

I skimmed the article about my dad. All the usual stuff about his movie credits. All the usual stuff about Aunt Izzy's first documentary winning an Academy Award, the usual stuff about Dad drinking too much, getting arrested before I was born. I got sick of reading the same thing over and over again. I always liked to see if there was anything about me or Mom.

Sure enough, there it was, how he met Mom on the set of their first movie together. How she inspired him to stop drinking. How when she got pregnant (Me! That was me!), he went to rehab because he didn't want to mess anything up with me.

But then…the article talked about Mom's cancer. There was a picture of Mom looking all skinny with her big alien eyes and fuzzy head. It made the baloney go cold again.

So did the pictures from her funeral. I knew paparazzi followed Dad all over the place, but they'd been at the *funeral?* No way. There were two pictures with me in them, with my swelled up cheeks, punched eyes, and dark teeth. Great. Photographic evidence that beautiful Annabeth Anderson and gorgeous Caleb Carlisle's daughter was a huge, fat, hideous beast. I hated the photographers. I thought about that day; it'd been horrible enough without them. I didn't want to know that someone else was there. It felt like someone seeing something really private, like they'd spied on me in the bathroom.

"So," Dad said, there in the kitchen, "are you going to talk to me about the stealing?"

"I said I was sorry!" I tried to scream. My throat felt scalded. The tears spilled over in my eyes. I tossed the magazine down on the counter. It landed face down in some lime juice.

Dad turned the magazine over. That little photo of his face was all wet. Some lime pulp stuck to the corner of his left eye.

He wiped his own photo with his fingertips. He looked down at his picture and said, "Listen, your spring break is coming up. You think you'd like to go out to Ohio? Stay with your aunt?"

"You just want to get rid of me! You hate me! You think I'm fat and ugly!"

Dad *closed his eyes!* I couldn't believe it. He shut his eyes like I was annoying him.

Fine. While he had his eyes closed, I grabbed that Ho Hos bag and ran up the stairs. I shut my door, then moved the desk in front of it. Dad couldn't stop me now. Nobody could. If Mom came back, I might be normal. If she hadn't known this horrible thing about me, maybe she wouldn't have died. If Dad quit drinking and everything was like it used to be, I could stop this.

But I knew there was no stopping me now. My stalker of a Secret Remedy was in control.

Chapter 9

I unzipped my jeans and yanked out the packet of lunch meat. I clawed at it, ripping it finally with my teeth. I pulled three slices out of the pack, wadded them in a ball and shoved it in my mouth. *Slow down, slow down,* I warned myself, terrified of how I nearly choked one night, how I had to do the Heimlich on my chair after my eyes filled up with black dots. That panicked me so bad I swore I'd never do it again. That was two days before. I'd done it twice since then. Once already that morning, before Dad finally emerged from his room.

My eyes watered as I pictured myself in my cafeteria job: hiding in the corner of the school kitchen, standing over the trash can, shoveling other people's leftovers into my mouth: bitten-into pizza crusts, tater tots, the corn and lima beans everyone left behind. I guzzled the remains of milkshakes, I licked plates clean of mashed potatoes, I scraped the pretzel cheese off the wax paper with my teeth. I devoured the fries no one else ate—the gray ones, the burnt ones, the weird tiny withered ones. I stood there in my hairnet and ate their trash like some dog.

I pulled another wad of baloney from the packet with my teeth. Saltiness registered on my tongue but by that point it was mostly texture, motion. Another slice shoved in. The packet had juice, water from the meat that I slurped off the plastic. I pulled out the candy bar, soft and mushy. I ripped it open and gnawed it off the wrapper, chewing baloney and chocolate together in my mouth. Then, the rest of the Ho Hos. A rhythm of

rip open,

shove in,

chew,

swallow,

rip open,

shove in,

chew,

swallow,

rip open,

shove in,

chew,

swallow.

I chugged half the bottle of water, then crawled to my

drawer, my secret stash. What this drawer held could be the end, all I had. I'd eaten everything I'd stolen from our kitchen freezer earlier, all those Tupperware containers of peanut chicken, coconut soup, and pasta salads that the cleaning lady had packed up and put away after the funeral. All the boxes of fancy soups, rolls of crackers, and jars of pesto I'd snuck from our pathetic cupboards. The mustard, the maple syrup, the chocolate sauce. I knew I should ration, but I knew I wouldn't. Once a binge began, I would eat every last scrap. I opened the drawer and devoured a loaf of bread, a pack of pudding cups, a box of oatmeal cream pies.

Finally, it happened.

Like a motor coming on, like a switch. The trance. I closed my eyes. I didn't need to see. I didn't taste. I didn't feel texture.

I didn't feel anything.

★★★

The knocking jerked me out of my stupor. Laila's voice at my door, barricaded by my desk. "Hannah? Dinner's ready."

I panted. Tears leaked down my face.

I ran my tongue around my mouth, then cleared my throat. "I-I'm not hungry."

"Are you okay, hon?" she asked. "Your dad said you argued."

"I'm fine," I croaked. "Thanks. I-I'm just not hungry. I feel kind of sick."

"You let me know if you need anything. I hope you'll come down later."

After a moment, I called, "Laila?" but she didn't answer. She'd gone away. *Good.*

My stomach groaned, bloated and miserable, with all those Ho Hos, baloney slices, and cupcakes sloshing around. *Cupcakes.*

The blue icing!

I'd better hurry. I gathered the empty bread bag, the pudding cups, all the wrappers and shoved them under the bed.

I made sure the room looked fine, and only then did I move my desk. This was the scariest part. If I got caught now, I wouldn't be able to finish.

I opened the door slowly. Voices drifted up from downstairs. Good. A sound buffer.

My pulse throbbed in my swollen fingertips as I tiptoed to the bathroom and locked the door.

I turned on the faucet just a little more than a trickle, so it made a noise if you were right outside the door, but not so you could hear it downstairs. From the cupboard under the sink I pulled out the box of tampons. I unwrapped one and put the pink wrapper on top of the pile of Kleenex in the wastebasket, shoving the unused tampon in my pocket. Mom and Dad had thought the toilet at home was clogged because I flushed tampons, so after that, I tried to always leave them as an excuse. I lifted the toilet lid, then the seat. It smelled, just faintly, of bleach.

I leaned over. I slipped my right two fingers into my mouth to touch the back of my throat.

The surge happened fast, but it happened long. I dreaded those seconds of suspension, those seconds where I couldn't breathe. But those horrible, eyes-bugged-out-throat-burning seconds had to happen to get to the release.

The release was this great rush, like when you're really scared of something, but then you find out it's okay, and that zippy feeling tingles in your fingers and ears, behind your knees, on top of your skull, and you feel alive and happy like you might laugh for a long time.

I gasped in breath and put a hand on the wall so I didn't fall down. No blue in the toilet. I didn't think so. Not this early. I couldn't flush yet. I only got so many flushes before people got suspicious. I'd never done this with Dad sober and with company in the house.

The tingles tickled my neck and scalp. Once I'd caught my breath, I bent over and tapped the back of my throat again. I kept my eyes open as I vomited. I needed to see the colors.

After round two, I leaned against the wall. Still no blue. I closed my eyes. The zippy feeling was good, but left me wobbly.

I counted to twenty, whispering the numbers, moving my tingling lips and thick tongue, then stood and vomited again. There it was—traces of bright blue floating in the slosh.

A fourth time—only hints of blue—and then I flushed.

When I stood, sparkling lights danced all over the bathroom walls. I blinked hard to bring the toilet back into focus. The water rose high, scaring me, then went down, fast and strong.

I kept blinking, but the room blurred wavy, the walls and floor melting together. I knelt, not sure I could keep standing, and leaned my forehead against the toilet seat.

I closed my eyes and savored the tingling, the shivers like giggles, reminding me of the runner's high I used to get. But worrying kept me from really flying.

I'd eaten all my secret stash. Dad would never let me out of his sight in a grocery store again. I'd already been written up for arriving to my after-lunch class flushed and watery-eyed. If they thought I was on drugs it wouldn't be too long before they'd start checking on me in the bathroom. I couldn't find where Dad was hiding his cash anymore. He was shipping me off to Aunt Izzy who was not clueless and knew my entire bag of tricks. What would I *do?*

My nose ran. I sniffed, but it didn't stop. When I opened my eyes, I watched dark beads of blood slide down the white porcelain bowl, leaving tainted trails behind.

Chapter 10

I had no reasons to be happy.

Dad and I hardly spoke to each other. After six in the evening, he wouldn't remember if we'd had a conversation anyway, so there didn't seem much point. He didn't *act* drunk; it's not like he fell down or slurred his speech, but he'd just sit and stare, tears in his eyes.

I spent a lot of time going through my mom's closet, taking the things that smelled the most like her lemon meringue lotion—a pink cashmere hoodie, a thin white nightgown, her pillowcase. I slept with these items. Sometimes, when I felt the SR tugging on me, I could talk myself out of it by inhaling her lemon scent.

Sometimes.

On nights I couldn't sleep, I'd shut off our alarm system and stand among my cities in the moonlight. I hadn't finished the last city for my mother. I hadn't gotten thin so she could see me beautiful just once before she died.

Aunt Izzy had reminded us of Mom's favorite saying when she gave the eulogy. Pretty is as pretty does.

I was a big, fat failure for my gorgeous mother.

After two weeks, I went back to school.

I walked into the building barely functional, feeling like I glowed neon. The expectation of being stared at made me long to crawl into a locker and hide. That new expectation added to the burden of being on guard for the B-Squad and gauging their reaction to me. Was I still "in"? Was I being released yet? I was so tense, my neck spasmed.

"What is *that?*" the familiar, poisonous voice hissed in my ear. "What is she *wearing?*"

I turned to Brooke, who looked past me down the hall at Kelly, a girl from our class Brooke didn't deem fashionable enough; Kelly wore a cute vintage dress with a puffy skirt, along with a pair of black high-tops.

Those were Brooke's first words to me after I returned from my mother's death and funeral. *What is that?* As if she were looking at rotten food on the sidewalk.

Kelly turned toward Brooke's voice, then flushed red. When Kelly walked away, the B-Squad collapsed into gales of laughter.

"Eww!" Brittany said, shaking her hands the way somebody might if they had bugs on them. "That was *so* gross! Did she like make that dress herself?"

"How could you go out looking like that?" Bebe asked.

"Does she *own* a mirror?" Brooke said.

The piano music flowed over my anxious body like a hot shower. I'd *missed* the piano music. I wanted to listen to something beautiful. Not this nasty noise.

I walked around the corner into the lounge, the B-Squad following me.

Jasper saw me and stopped playing. "Hey, Hannah," he said. "How are you doing?"

His voice, his words, rolled over me just like his music. "I'm okay. Thanks. For asking."

The B-Squad stared.

Jasper stood up. "I'm so sorry. About your mom." That yellow slice in his eye shimmered.

"Thank you," I whispered. My eyes burned, and I knew I was going to cry again. I turned away from the girls and ducked into a bathroom. *Maybe they'd follow me, comfort me, and apologize for not asking how I was.*

They didn't.

I wasn't surprised.

In health class, Mrs. DeTello hugged me. "Good to have you back. How are you?"

I'm a train wreck, I wanted to tell her. *I'm out of control and it scares me. My dad is unraveling. Please help me.*

But I just nodded and whispered, "I'm okay."

DeTello told us about a major project we'd be starting after Spring Break. She was telling us early so we could start it "percolating in our brains." We were all going to have to complete a "Make a Difference" Project, where we created some kind of service project to make a difference in our world. She stressed that there were many different kinds of "worlds": "You could interpret the word to mean your immediate family," she said, "or your neighborhood, or the school, this community, the city, some other city, the nation, another nation. Think outside the box and come up with a project that means something to *you* personally."

This assignment wrapped me in that lead blanket again, just like in the counselor's office. *Make a difference? Who, me? Right. Like that's gonna happen.*

Later, I got called out of science to go down to the principal's office. Suarez offered me condolences, assured me the teachers would be understanding if I struggled a bit, and let me know I didn't have to work in the cafeteria anymore.

I panicked.

No, that's an understatement. I actually had a meltdown right there in her office. I *had* to work in the cafeteria! What would I do without it? I *begged* her to let me still do it. Suarez must've thought I was crazy. I tried to convince her I couldn't stand for anything else to change right now. I got her to agree, but I wouldn't be surprised if I got summoned to the counselor again soon.

I *needed* the lunch duty. That's what was keeping me alive.

Jasper and the kitchen staff gave me a card they'd all signed. Pam and the others all wrote really sweet, real things. I got teary-eyed again, but it made me feel *good*. In the kitchen, with those people, was the only place I felt human.

In geography, we watched a video about the diamond mines in Sierra Leone. There were all these kids with missing arms or ears or eyes. Rebels had hacked them off with machetes to "send a message."

I closed my eyes. I thought of Aunt Izzy and her documentary. I knew she'd interviewed orphans in Sierra Leone. *Aunt Izzy. Aunt Izzy. You've got to save me.*

I lay in bed breathing my mother's pink cardigan, seething

at my dad "sleeping" on the couch, and actually thought, *if I were missing an arm or an eye, no one would expect anything from me.* If I'd shown up at school with some kind of handicap, the B-Squad would never have given me the time of day. I might still be the authentic Hannah.

Chapter 11

38. Chocolate-dipped strawberries

39. Rock climbing

40. The way ducks sound like they're chuckling

41. The scent of vanilla

42. Revenge movies

43. The word "peevish" (I just like it)

44. Manatees

45. The way patriotic marches played by whole orchestras make me feel like I'm going to cry

I sat on the plane, on my way to Ohio, flipping through the list I'd started way back in seventh grade. I hadn't added anything to my purple book since the blue icing day. I tried to think of something to be happy about: getting away from Dad (but that didn't count because he'd forced me to go), getting away from the B-Squad...but those weren't things worthy of my list. They were only temporary reasons. I needed *real* ones.

Starting a new adventure?

Please. Brooke would laugh at that. I was going to *Ohio*. What kind of an adventure could I possibly have in Ohio, I could hear her mocking.

Brooke was going to the Bahamas for the two-week vacation. Brittany was going to her condo in St. Thomas, and Bebe to Mexico City. Me? I was being banished to Ohio. Woo-hoo.

There were two saving graces in the B-Squad's eyes: Aunt Izzy won an Academy Award for her last documentary *Need*, which was about addiction. Even though none of those losers watches documentaries—they'd think I was an even bigger geek if they knew I loved them. *Watching documentaries* is #76 on the list—an Oscar is an Oscar and carries clout. That and the fact that Izzy was in an inpatient program for eating disorders when she was in high school. (I didn't tell them that—they knew because it's always in the coverage about my mom and dad.)

"Cool," Brooke said, with wide, admiring eyes as we waited for algebra to start. "That's hardcore. That's serious."

I nodded.

"Maybe," Brooke said, "she could teach you a thing or two."

I thought my face would explode.

"Ouch, Brooke," Bebe said, but her eyes were bright and gleeful.

Brittany just stared down at her book.

My eyes burned. *Don't cry, don't cry, don't cry.* I could not bleed for these sharks.

"Oh, for God's sake, lighten up," Brooke said. I wasn't sure if she was talking to me or Bebe. "I just meant that your aunt really knows what she's doing, if she had to go into a hospital. Wouldn't we all love to be anorexic? I just meant that you'll be with a master, so pay attention. Bring some tips back for the rest of us."

When the plane finally took off, my chest convulsed as I fought not to cry. I missed my mom. I should've been nicer to my dad. I should've stayed home to help take care of him. I shouldn't be such a monumental screw-up. If I was a normal, good daughter, he'd want me around.

Dad had been scaring me lately. I hated that he scared me—a father's supposed to comfort you. He drank way too much. He forgot to do basic stuff at the house, like buy groceries and have the grass cut, and his publicist and assistant were around a lot more than they used to be, doing things like picking me up from school, doing our laundry, and bringing me takeout dinners. Sean and Laila had become a daily presence too, and I knew they were as scared as I was because they were both *way* too cheerful and perky all the time.

Kevin stopped me in the hall the other day. He'd grabbed my arm, hard, and said, really close to my face, "Your drunk dad better not wreck my movie."

"You better not wreck *his* movie," I shot back, but the taste of rust rushed through me. Was my dad falling apart enough to derail a film? What Dad did in our house was one thing. What he did in front of my classmates was another.

L.A. disappeared from view in its perpetual brown smog. We rose above it to pink cotton candy clouds. When the sky looked like a field of snow, I closed my eyes.

I wanted to hurl myself out of the exit door when I remembered the conversation I'd overheard at home. Aunt Izzy called the landline and Dad and I both picked up at the same second in different parts of the house. He spoke first, and even though I hadn't deliberately planned to do it, I stayed on the line, feeling more horrible and creepy with everything they said.

Aunt Izzy got right to her point. "When are you going to get Hannah in treatment?"

Dad sighed. "Izzy, you never quit."

"This is urgent, Caleb. You can't ignore it. You both need help."

"What's next, Iz? You going to tell me *I'm* anorexic?"

"I'm talking about your daughter. Your daughter who is in a lot of pain."

"Of course she's in pain! Her mother just died! That doesn't mean—Izzy, you think *everyone* has an eating disorder. It's just your thing."

"When have I *ever* suggested that someone else had an eating disorder?"

"You just—you just, I mean, come on, Izzy, Hannah's *overweight*."

I feared they'd hear my intake of breath from that punch to the gut.

"You've never said that to her, have you?" She sounded like she might kick him if she could.

"Well, not so bluntly...but, yeah. Annabeth...and I talked to her about it." Dad tripped on my mom's name.

"Oh, Caleb, she's in trouble. The stealing at school, the shoplifting, all of it is related."

Dad groaned. "Please. She just wants attention."

"Of *course* she wants attention!" Aunt Izzy snapped. "Her mother just died!"

Silence. I bet my dad felt punched in the stomach too.

"Think about it," Izzy said. "All she wants is attention, Caleb, and is she getting any from you or are you—"

She didn't finish, but I knew what she was going to say and I knew my dad did too, because I'd heard them argue about it before. *Or are you just drunk all the time?*

That's when I'd hung up.

A lot of good my little secret friend did me.

But still, the SR was as close to a real friend as I had. I actually pictured her as a person.

At least she never betrayed me like my breathing, living friends did. I probably shouldn't even *call* them friends. I probably only did because otherwise I'd have to face the pathetic fact that no one who actually existed liked me.

There *had* been someone who actually existed who'd liked me.

Or maybe not *liked* me, but treated me like a human being. But I'd destroyed that the day before. It wasn't enough that I'd said I didn't like him in front of a whole art room of people. Or that I'd told him I liked Kevin. No, I had to make it worse.

Oh God. I shrunk down farther in my seat, wishing I could curl in on myself and disappear. Jasper'd *seen* me. He'd seen me on a binge. It *hurt* me to remember the look on his face.

I'd been standing in the corner by a trash can, in the tiny room between the kitchen and the cafeteria, the room where the doors could open for the delivery trucks. I stood there scarfing down trash—a bunch of grilled cheese sandwiches we hadn't sold, about seven of them, one after the other—and a sound had made me turn.

The sound had been Jasper. *Oh God, the look on his face.* He was appalled. Horrified.

I froze, my mouth full, my cheeks stuffed out, grease and crumbs all over my face I'm sure.

"Hannah?" He asked it like he wasn't even sure it was me.

I couldn't chew. I couldn't swallow. I couldn't speak. I couldn't breathe.

"What are—are-are you okay?" he whispered.

A whole year passed before he moved. He stepped toward me and I bolted. I dropped the grilled cheese sandwich in my hand and ran. I ran to the bathroom and threw up, then I ran outside. I just ran and ran and ran. I ran until I got lost and had to leave a panicked message on my dad's voice mail.

Laila came to pick me up. When she hugged me, I tried not to cry.

"Where's my dad?" I asked, missing the smell and hug of my own mother.

Laila looked away and said, "He's working, hon, so he called me."

I knew she lied. What, was he too busy to be bothered if I was lost and wandering L.A.?

Maybe Sean and Laila could adopt me. They didn't have any kids of their own.

I wasn't brave enough to ask her, though.

Maybe the plane would be hijacked by terrorists. Maybe we would crash. Maybe I'd never have to deal with Brooke or Brittany or Bebe or Kevin or any of them again.

But then…I'd never see Jasper again.

I'd never see *Dad* again. I thought about my dad at another funeral. That wounded defeat in his eyes at Mom's. The desperate way he'd held my hand through the whole thing.

Okay, plane, I take it back. Don't go down.

I was nervous for the rest of the flight, afraid I'd jinxed us with my thought.

Chapter 12

Reasons to Be Happy:

None.

My dad got arrested.

Again.

He's all over the news and Internet, even here in Ohio. I'd been here for one week already. Things were actually going well. Aunt Izzy was awesome. She was letting me log videotape on her Africa documentary. We were having a blast.

Well, except for the fact that for four days, Dad hadn't answered my emails or calls. I just thought he was tired of pretending he cared enough to talk to me. Tired of listening to me blather on about canoeing on the Little Miami, climbing at the Urban Krag, taking Latin Dance class at El Meson, or having a picnic on the lawn of the Dayton Art Institute.

Then came the morning when Aunt Izzy came into my room while it was still dark. She sat on the edge of my bed in a T-shirt and yoga pants, her hair still all messed up. "Hannah Banana," she whispered, "I have some bad news, sweetie."

Dad had been drunk. He'd been drunk for days, apparently, and hadn't shown up for work on the vampire movie. He'd crashed our Land Rover into a rental car of tourists from Indianapolis. One of them had to go to the hospital with a broken arm, but the rest were okay except for needing some stitches. Both cars were trashed. The pictures in the paper made me feel sick.

They'd been on the Pacific Coast Highway.

All the times we'd driven that highway, all the times I'd thought *just one wrong move and we'd end up in the ocean.* He could've fallen over the cliff, been trapped in his car, and drowned.

He could've killed that whole family from Indiana.

His mug shot was hideous.

I bet Brooke wouldn't say he was hot when she saw *that* picture of him. He looked like he actually *was* a vampire—so pale with black circles around his eyes, cheeks all gaunt, eyes bloodshot. It hurt me to look at him so *ashamed* and small.

He'd spent the night in jail. Who wants to picture their dad in a jail? In an ugly blue jumpsuit? With maybe a scary cell mate? I couldn't sleep I was so terrified for him.

His publicist had called Aunt Izzy. So had Sean and Laila.

Dad hadn't talked to either one of us yet. As much as I wanted him to call, I had no idea what I'd say to him. What could you say after something like that?

What was *everyone else* saying?

Oh my God, how could I go to school and face Brooke and the B-Squad? Dad was the only thing I had going for me.

The confusion made me feel sick; I wanted to kick Dad at the same time I wanted to hide him away somewhere and protect him.

Aunt Izzy understood how freaked I was. "What do you need to do?" she asked.

I knew what I needed, but I couldn't tell her that. With my SR, I wouldn't have to feel anything. It would take away all this panic.

My SR wasn't so secret. Aunt Izzy talked about it all the time. She called it what it was.

I couldn't stand to be in my hot, itchy skin, but I held it together most of that first day.

Aunt Izzy took me to Sugarcreek, this great nature preserve. We'd gone there with my mom once years ago. They'd taken me to see the Three Sisters, these enormous oak trees that were over six hundred years old. Me, Mom, and Aunt Izzy together couldn't wrap our arms around *one* of the trunks, that's how big they were.

That day, when we climbed up to them, my eyes filled with tears and my back started shaking. Aunt Izzy put her arm around me, but I shrugged it off, hard.

"Don't touch me," I said.

She nodded. She didn't seem mad.

"I can't stand to be in my own body," I whispered. "I want—"

"What?"

"I wish I could zip it off, my own skin. I want to run. I want to run *really* hard."

"So run. You know where the car is. I won't leave without you."

I left her standing there at the Three Sisters and I ran as fast as I could, more like fleeing. Like I was running *from* something. But, the problem is, you can't run away from yourself. It felt good anyway, to sweat and breathe hard. Made the panicky swirl in my chest spin less.

The muscles in my thighs and *fat butt* warmed up, then burned, as I kept running running running on the muddy trails.

When I'd been on the track team, I almost always won.

I missed track. I missed losing myself in the laps. It would've been a comfort. It was a comfort as I ran all the way down to the big wide creek—the actual Sugar Creek the place was named for—before I slowed to a walk, panting. I'd run almost three miles without stopping. Not bad for not having trained for over a year. I clutched my side and gasped for air.

Maybe if I wasn't so fat, Dad wouldn't drink so much. Maybe if I wasn't so gross and had to shoplift and do my disgusting habit, I'd still be in my own home and Dad would be fine and working and we'd be sad without Mom but okay.

What was going to happen to me now?

I limped my way back to the car where Aunt Izzy sat on the hood, cross-legged, leaning back, looking at the sky. She looked all content, like she would've waited all day for me.

We went to dinner at the greatest restaurant, The Winds, which we could walk to from Izzy's cool purple house. Later that night, while she and her assistant Pearl discussed something in her office, I loaded my gym bag full of food from her cupboards and fridge. She'd stocked the house with all my favorite things which I shoved into the bag: a loaf of rye bread, a roll of sugar cookie dough, slices of provolone cheese, sliced turkey, the leftover chicken enchiladas we'd made last night, the leftover guacamole, the pasta salad, the tapioca pudding.

I hid the bag in my room. After Pearl left, we went to bed. I lay awake until I was certain Aunt Izzy was asleep.

It took over me again. It had been so long. Well, long for me anyway. I almost wept with relief, it felt so good, so comforting.

The trance took over.

I stopped feeling.

No shame. No worries.

Nothing. Lovely, wonderful *nothing*.

But the nothing didn't last. When I came back to myself, my stomach strained with all I'd forced into it. Sharp pains stabbed me as I crawled to my feet, clutching my belly, and snuck to the hallway bathroom. Aunt Izzy had her own bathroom in her bedroom. Since her bedroom door was shut, I thought I was pretty safe.

I quietly closed the bathroom door and turned on the light. I looked repulsive in the mirror, my face so bloated, a smear of something dark on my chin. I turned away.

I rubbed my bloated gut. Revolting. Vile.

I lifted the lid on her toilet and went through my ritual.

Once.

Twice.

Then flushed.

Ah, there it was.

Relief.

Twice more.

The tingles began. The floating. Numbness tickling my fingers and toes.

Now. Now, maybe I could sleep.

But the sliding sensation began deep inside my face. Red splatters fell on the toilet seat, startling against the white porcelain. I snatched up a handful of toilet paper to plug up my nose, then used my other hand to try to clean up the mess.

I sat on the floor, leaning my head back against the tub.

The helium-light floatiness faded away. Queasy shakiness took over. The nosebleeds ruined everything and they were happening *every time!* My limbs trembled. This sucked.

By the time I got the bleeding to stop, my head throbbed like someone played a drum inside it. My arms and legs had a heavy flu-like stiffness.

I avoided the mirror, ducking my head as I passed it to open the door.

Aunt Izzy sat on the floor in the hall.

She sat there in flannel pajama bottoms and a tattered sweatshirt. She had the same I-could-wait-forever air about her, just like when I had gone running that day—was that just earlier that same day? Was my life really crawling along so painfully slowly? A spray bottle of disinfectant cleaner and a rag sat near her left hand.

"Feel better?" she asked, squinting up at me in the light.

Was this a trap? But she asked it kindly, no judgment in her voice.

"I know it was a hard day," she said, her voice even and calm. "I know that the bingeing and purging is an old standby in tough times. I have to be on the lookout for my own self-destructive habits when I'm having a rough time."

My jaw dropped. "You...you knew what I was doing?"

She shrugged, her expression one of *hello, of course I knew what you were doing*.

"Why didn't you try to stop me?" I wanted to *kick* her. "You should've tried to stop me!"

Izzy shook her head. "You have to stop it. Not me."

Unsteady, I stared down at her.

She gestured to the cleaning supplies beside her. "I understand you're going to do this. You know we all want you to stop, but sometimes it's going to happen. When it does you'll need to clean up after yourself, okay? You have to take responsibility for your habits."

I stood there with my mouth open like a cartoon of a girl in shock.

"It's okay," Aunt Izzy said. "You can get over this. I've been there, sweetie, I know."

"You were...bulimic?" The word was bug spray in my mouth.

She shook her head. "Nope. That wasn't my thing."

I leaned against the wall, then slid down it across from her. "I wish I were anorexic! How did you *do* it? I wish I could do it!"

Aunt Izzy's face pinched up like she'd smelled rotting garbage. "*What?* Why would you say something so stupid?" Her mean, harsh tone slapped my face. She'd *never* called me stupid.

Tears scalded my eyes. "I-I just meant that..."

But Aunt Izzy's eyes were bright, like she had a fever. "You just meant *what?*"

"I want to be thin. I-I just want to be pretty. A-and anorexia is *better*. It's not so disgusting. If I could only pull it off, I—"

Aunt Izzy was on her feet so fast, it scared me. She yanked me up by the arm and pulled me down the hall, her nails digging into my skin.

She opened the attic door and turned on the light. She didn't release my arm until we were at the top of the stairs. The rough wooden floor chilled my bare feet. She dug around in a couple of boxes, muttering under her breath. When she found the one she wanted, she hefted it up from behind some tubs of Christmas decorations. She dropped it into the dust at our feet, where it hit with a heavy *whump*. "Sit."

I did.

She opened the box and handed me a manila envelope. "Open it. Take a look."

I undid the envelope's clasp. A pile of 5x7 black-and-white photographs slid into my lap. I frowned, then brought the top photo closer to my face in the weird light. It was Aunt Izzy, as a girl, standing naked except for a pair of panties. She looked like someone in a concentration camp, like those documentaries we'd watched before we started reading *Anne Frank: The Diary of a Young Girl*. My nose wrinkled. She was a *skeleton*; every single rib stood out in stark relief, her hip bones protruded like shovels, her elbows and knees were grapefruit-sized knots, wider than her stick thighs and arms.

"*That's* not disgusting?" Aunt Izzy asked.

The next photo was a back view. Her shoulder blades were alien wings. Every vertebrae in her spine bumped out like a pop-bead necklace embedded under her skin. At the end of that spine...I peered closer.

"Looks like a tail, doesn't it?" Her voice cut me with its

iciness. "Look at how scabbed and gross my tailbone is. I got bruises just from sitting in a chair."

My post-purge headache throbbed behind my left eye.

She took the stack of photos from me and shuffled them, handing me another, a close-up of the empty bowl of her stomach and another of her face. "You don't think that's disgusting? You'd actually *wish* for that? I look like some circus freak! I couldn't create internal heat anymore. Your body tries to protect you, so it grows *fur*." There it was on her belly and cheeks, white fur like a cat's pelt. "Yeah, that's *really* pretty, isn't it?"

In the photo, the skull under her transparent, mummy-like skin was clearly defined, her eyes sunk in their cavernous sockets. The grain of her facial muscles was visible, like an anatomical model for science class. The intersection of cartilage turning to bone in her nose was as sharp as two pieces set together in a puzzle.

Most of her crown was bald, and other bald patches showed through her thin hair.

"You look like Mom," I whispered. "After chemo."

Aunt Izzy's voice lost that nasty, hard edge. "Just think, your mom lost her hair fighting to save her life, and I lost mine basically trying to kill myself."

I looked up at her, not sure I understood.

"My body started to cannibalize itself," she said. "My heart. My brain. I've got an irregular heartbeat because of those years, did you know that? I stopped having periods because I was so malnourished. I didn't produce enough estrogen for my bones, so now I have these brittle, old-lady bones. I can't run anymore because I get stress fractures. But, hey, I was thin, right?"

I'd thought Mom was too thin at the end, but she'd looked downright hearty, even in her last days, compared to these pictures.

"I couldn't see myself at all," Izzy said, flipping through the photos in her hand. "I would do anything to lose weight. *Anything*. Once, my therapist even asked me if I'd cut off an arm or leg to weigh less and I said *yes*. That's...that's just obscene to me now."

I thought about that Sierra Leone video and what I'd wished.

Aunt Izzy shuffled through the photos some more. She stopped at one picture, putting her hand over her mouth.

I took the photo from her. Her face looked like she'd gone through a windshield. Her left eye was dark where it should be white, and the bruised lid stretched huge and puffy. The entire left side of her face was swollen to twice its size, and along her shaved hairline a row of stitches looked like barbed wire against her white scalp.

"I passed out in the shower," she said. "Your mother found me lying there bleeding."

I burst into tears picturing my mother young, frightened… *still alive.*

Izzy scooted closer to me on that splintery attic floor, wrapping her arms around me.

"I *want* to stop," I cried. "I really do. I don't know *how.* She won't leave me alone!"

Aunt Izzy leaned back so she could look in my face. "Who won't leave you alone?"

My stomach fluttered. "I didn't mean a person, I just—I don't know how…I don't want to…do that"—I'd never said the words "binge" or "purge"; they made it seem too real—"but then, it's like it tells me that nothing will make me feel as good as it can."

Aunt Izzy's eyes were bright. "So the bulimia? You referred to the bulimia as a person. You said, 'She won't leave me alone.' Do you think of her as a person?"

I hesitated. Would she think I was certifiably insane?

Before I could answer, she said, "I did that. I still kind of do. I started thinking of anorexia as a person. That was her name, you know, like she was this girl I actually knew called Anorexia."

My heart lifted. I nodded.

"It's like I could…picture her." Aunt Izzy drew her knees up to her chest. "I used to think she was beautiful, so tall and willowy, with this pearly white skin and big eyes, but now… now I see her for who she truly is. Some kind of monster. She's got fangs and these long limbs that are too bendy to be a real person's."

Wow.

"So," she asked me, "what does Bulimia look like?"

"I-I used to think she was pretty too, but now…she's short. And pudgy. She has bloodshot eyes and rotten teeth. And really frizzy, fried hair."

Aunt Izzy laughed. "That's good. That's great. It's *not* crazy, you know, to picture them. Especially to picture them as monsters. They are *not* our friends. They want to kill us."

Tears surprised me—for real, I didn't know I was going to cry again. "But…"

"There are no buts in this, Hannah! Bulimia could rupture your esophagus and you could bleed to death out of your mouth. That'd be a pretty way to go, huh? Or she could stop your heart. She could be making your bones brittle too. When was the last time you had a period?"

I shrugged. I couldn't remember. "I can't be malnourished," I said. "I'm fat."

"You are *not* fat."

"I am too! My face is all pudgy, and I'm gaining—"

"You know who made your face pudgy? Bulimia. All of this"—she cupped my ridiculous giant cheeks in her hands—"is your salivary glands. They're swollen. They're desperate. They're working overtime to absorb any bit of nutrition from you at all before you puke it up."

I flinched. It sounded so ugly, so harsh. And *wasn't* it?

She touched her fingers to my face. "Your eyes, your beautiful eyes, look like you've been in a fight. No amount of makeup can hide those dark circles. It's from the pressure when you vomit. Eventually, you start busting those blood vessels. And your teeth, they're so dark. She's rotting your teeth with all that stomach acid."

"Shut up!" I said. "Stop it, just stop. Are you trying to make me hate myself?"

Aunt Izzy stroked my hair. "No, sweetie, I'm not. I think you're doing just fine at that on your own."

Chapter 13

Reasons to Be Happy:

Nope, still can't think of any.

I wanted to hate Aunt Izzy, but I couldn't. She told the truth.

I hadn't told the truth in a long time.

Neither had my mom. Or my dad.

Certainly not any of my "friends."

Please. The only friends I had were a completely made up rotten-toothed demon and a bunch of backstabbing gossips.

What about Jasper? I'd been mean to him just to please the B-Squad. And then I'd grossed him out. He may have been my friend once, but I'd put a big fat stop to that.

I didn't get to talk to my dad for three more days, and when I did, it was an excruciating phone call. His misery seemed like a stream of black spray paint hissing on the phone line between us, so strong and real I thought I could catch it in my hand. I imagined it would burn me, leaving charred spots on my palms. I didn't blame him for the shame, but it's painful to hear your own dad like that. What was I supposed to say? My father, my only parent left alive, was as big a loser as I was.

"Hannah, I'm so sorry. I'm so sorry."

"It's okay, Dad."

Why did I say that? It *wasn't* okay, but I didn't know any other answer.

"I've been so sad," he said, "and I haven't dealt with my grief. That's not an excuse, but…"

But that's your excuse.

Just like it's mine.

"It's okay," I repeated.

"I'm…what I've done is unforgivable. I can't…I can't go on like this. I need help."

Hello? Just call him Sherlock.

"I'm going to go into a rehab program."

"Oh. Okay. Are you still in the movie?"

"I…um, I don't think so, no."

Kevin's hateful voice floated into my brain. *Your drunk dad better not wreck my movie.*

120

There was a long, tortured pause.

"So," I said, determined to make this call I'd wished for last longer than two minutes, "are you okay? Were you hurt…in the wreck?"

"I'm okay. I…have some stitches in my chin…thank God nobody was seriously hurt."

I'd read in the newspaper that he was paying all the medical bills for the Indianapolis tourists.

"I'm glad too, Dad. What…um, what will you do in rehab?"

I could almost *see* him squirming. We were out of practice at being so honest. It was hard. "I'll mostly have therapy, I guess. I need to learn to deal with, you know, my feelings, without covering them up with drinking."

My heart banged so loud in my skull it reminded me of the pounding from my horrible nosebleeds. I took a deep breath. "Daddy?" I hadn't called him that for years. It just floated out of my mouth, sounding too high and girly. "I-I think I need rehab too."

A long silence.

"Not for drinking," I said. "But for my…bulimia." I had to brace myself to say it out loud, and I swear, I could feel *him* brace, even with a thousand miles between us. "I need help."

"Have you been talking to your aunt about this?" His words were clipped, skeptical.

"Yes, but…Dad, this is for real. I don't want to do this anymore. I need help too."

"Honey, if you don't want to do that anymore, why don't you just *stop*?"

The cruelty of it took my breath away.

"I *can't* just stop, Dad. I've tried. I don't know *how*."

"It's a question of willpower, Hannah."

"Is that your problem too?" I asked. "No willpower?"

"Hannah, that's not fair. Addiction is a serious illness."

"So is bulimia!"

His sigh was so loaded with irritation it made me want to smash this phone down on his head. So *he* got to need help, but I didn't?

"Hannah, think about it: it's a choice. Why don't you just stop bingeing?"

"Why don't *you* just stop drinking?" I said.

Then I hung up.

★★★

I *hated* feeling mad at my dad. How did that happen? All I had wanted for a whole week was for him to call me! Then he did and what did I do? I had to get all nasty and mean. Of *course*, all I wanted to do after that call was binge. The anger buzzed like hornets trapped under my skin. I couldn't sit still. I paced the hallway. I started picturing it: how I could go fill up my gym bag with food from the cupboards while Aunt Izzy worked in her office.

My phone vibrated. It was Dad. I let it go to voice mail.

I went to the kitchen and made myself a cup of licorice tea. I stood at the sink and drank it.

Dad called again.

Then a third time. I still didn't answer.

The buzzing under my skin got worse. I circled the kitchen five times. I looked in the cupboards. There was plenty I could scrounge up for a binge. I reached for a box of Life cereal.

I put it back.

Come on. You know it will feel good. You're under so much stress.

I took the box back down. I opened it.

Think of it. Peace and quiet. Relief. Just something to release the pressure.

With trembling hands, I poured one bowl of cereal, then put the box back in the cupboard.

That's it? That's all? You expect that to help?

I poured milk over the cereal, got a spoon, and walked into the living room. I heard Aunt Izzy and Pearl talking in her office.

I sat on the couch and ate a bite of cereal.

You're not going to really just eat this, are you? What's the point? You could eat the whole box and feel better. And not have any of the calories. I thought you wanted to be skinny.

I picked up the remote and turned on the TV. Just to drown out the voice. I found a stupid *Where Are They Now?* program, publicly humiliating toppled celebrities. How long before my dad ended up on one of these shows?

Dad called back a fourth time. I ignored the phone, upped the volume on the TV, and ate my cereal, not even tasting it.

Then Aunt Izzy came out of her office, shutting the door behind her, on her cell phone. It didn't take me long to figure out through her one-sided conversation that she was talking to my dad. Guilt rushed through me for not taking his calls. What kind of daughter was I?

Aunt Izzy talked in the kitchen. When I heard my mother's name mentioned, I lowered the volume on the TV and strained my ears. I couldn't turn the volume off; it would be too obvious I was eavesdropping. I flipped through some channels, found something quieter, and tried to hear what Aunt Izzy said.

"Well, Annabeth can't be used as a real judge, though, because she never entirely understood it. It was always an issue between us."

What was she talking about?

"Yeah...right, right...she said that to me often...but, Caleb, there's nothing simple about eating reasonably to someone with an eating disorder. Just like there's nothing simple about drinking reasonably to an alcoholic."

She was quiet a long time. I froze, cereal spoon in my hand.

"It stops being about being thin. That's not the issue any more than the point of your drinking is to get drunk, am I right?"

Aunt Izzy wandered into the living room, noticed me there, and walked back into the kitchen. When she spoke again, I realized she'd gone up the stairs. I couldn't make out what she was saying anymore.

I looked down. My cereal bowl was empty. I didn't remember eating it. I got up and poured myself another. I flipped through channels until I returned to the *Where Are They Now?* show.

Pretty soon, Aunt Izzy's voice became audible again. "Of course. What about school?"

Was he asking for me to stay here? I wasn't sure how I felt about that. I didn't want to go home and face the train wreck of our lives, but I wanted Dad to *want* me there.

School. That meant Brooke and Brittany and Bebe. And

Kevin. My skin itched. The hornets buzzed. *You'd feel better. Just do it.*

"I leave for Ghana again next Wednesday," she said.

I'd forgotten about that. How long was Dad in rehab? If Aunt Izzy was out of the country and Dad was in rehab, where was I supposed to stay?

Suddenly, a blast of loud drum music blared from the office. *Really* loud drum music, with people singing in the background. When it stopped, I heard just a few syllables of Aunt Izzy in the kitchen before the exact same drum sequence played again.

Then a third time. Then a fourth.

"Perfect!" Pearl yelled from the office.

But by that point, Aunt Izzy was off the phone. She sat beside me on the couch.

"Didn't Dad want to talk to me?" I asked, sounding offended.

She pursed her lips into sort of a smile. "Oh, I think you made it pretty clear you didn't want to talk to *him*."

"Is he mad?"

"No. You made him listen. Good for you."

Before I could say anything else, though, she reached for the remote and shut off the TV. She gestured to my cereal bowl and said, "I'll let you in on the only eating tip you'll ever need. It's not a dieting tip. It's a life tip. When you eat something, just eat."

What? I cocked my head and raised my eyebrows, expecting more.

"When you're eating, only eat," she repeated. "Don't watch TV, don't read, don't drive. Just eat with your entire awareness. Taste every bite. Pay attention. Learn to listen to your body."

I wanted to say that was the stupidest thing I'd ever heard, but then I thought about that first bowl of cereal.

I looked down at the second bowl, half-eaten.

I wasn't hungry anymore, not really, but it was comforting to crunch the cereal. I liked how it felt in my mouth.

"I'm telling you," she said, "it's the simplest thing in the world. No one would be fat or anorexic or bulimic if we'd just learn to do that one thing. But, as you well know, simple and easy are two very different things."

I nodded. "How long will he be in rehab?"

She didn't seem bothered by my change in subject. "Twenty-eight days. At least."

"Does he have to live there, or does he go during the day?"

"He has to stay there. He's actually not allowed to leave. It was this or jail, Hannah."

Oh. I hadn't known that part.

"Did he say where I'm supposed to stay if you're leaving the country?"

"He has no idea, but how would you like to go to Africa?"

I froze. *He has no idea?* That terrified me. Was he no longer capable of the most basic things a father was supposed to do?

"He'll never let me go to Africa," I said, in a voice I hardly recognized. I said that instead of shouting, "I can't go to Africa! My dad needs me at home!"

Because he was supposed to need me, right?

Because he was supposed to want me to come home, right?

I didn't *want* to go to Africa.

I was scared of Africa.

How would I binge? How would I purge?

My dad would never let me go so far away from him, right?

Wrong.

Chapter 14

Eight days later, sitting in our hotel room as the sun rose on my first morning in Ghana, I dug my sequined purple notebook from my duffel bag.

I flipped through a few pages. Reasons to be happy? Please. More like reasons to be terrified:

1. My father doesn't want me around
2. My father is going to end up in jail
3. I have no real friends
4. I'm never going to get well
5. I'm in a third world country half a planet away from everything I know
6. I'll never be able to finish all the schoolwork I'm missing
7. I'll flunk and have to repeat my eighth grade year

8. That won't matter because I'll end up weighing five hundred pounds and won't be able to fit on the plane to go home

I am really, truly in Africa*!*

What am I doing *here?*

We'd arrived the night before. As we started to descend in Accra—Ghana's capital—it had just begun to get dark and the sky was red. For real red. Red like Chinese lanterns. Underneath all that red was a glittering coastline of lights. Like any other city in the world.

Stepping off the plane was total sensory overload that made it hard to breathe. What I *could* breathe had a distinct odor: meat cooking, sweat, animal musk, and a smoky aroma of something on the edge of burning. Mix all those ingredients with hot, humid, oily temperatures and you'll understand why the first whiff of Africa made me woozy.

We met Ben, our guide and driver. He's a big man with a lullaby voice. I attached myself to him like super glue, practically holding his hand.

When we stepped outside the airport, I saw men and woman dressed in modern trendy clothes, men and women in tribal dress, and everything in between. Of course, by that point, we'd been traveling for twenty-four hours. I was an overtired, overwhelmed, scaredy-cat zombie. When we got to the hotel, I practically passed out.

After waking, I looked across our hotel room; Aunt Izzy was still asleep, curled on her side, her back to me. I tried to be quiet as I sat cross-legged on my bed with my purple book and contemplated my list. I thought about putting *Not bingeing for three days*, but the list wasn't like that. It's only for things that *always* make me happy, not too specific to any certain time in my life.

I could've listed *Not having to go back to school* too. I didn't have to face the B-Squad and all their judgment about my dad, my fat butt, and my loserdom for a good long time. I had tons of homework to do while I was gone, though. I'd been freaked out when I'd seen the pile of stuff and instructions from my teachers. I knew Aunt Izzy had told my teachers what was going on with me—*all* of it, not just the Dad crisis. I could tell by the cheesy notes they wrote me. DeTello wrote me this great note, though, and said she only wanted me to do my Make a Difference Project, "Because I know Hannah Carlisle has a lot to offer the world." Hmm.

I could've also put *Starting therapy* on my list, but I wanted the list to stand on its own. Aunt Izzy got me an appointment in Yellow Springs with this woman Giulia Florio. Her first name is pronounced Julia but it's spelled that gorgeous

Italian way. She's freakishly tall, but stunning, with his huge beaky nose that makes her look exotic, and crazy hair with wild messy curls.

I liked her.

That surprised me. I went prepared to hate her. I'd hoped that maybe there'd be some magic cure, something Giulia would do or say to "fix" me right away. I'd been shocked that she'd hardly even mentioned bulimia the first couple of times. (I had gone eight days in a row. That was "highly unusual" my aunt and Giulia both told me, but since we were leaving the country, "these were extenuating circumstances.")

For the first few appointments, I actually felt guilty knowing how much they cost, when all Dr. Giulia did was talk about things I liked to do and asked about things I thought I was good at. We drank chai and chatted about my cities and running. We talked a *lot* about my mom and dad, but it wasn't until the fourth visit that she brought up bulimia at all.

At first, I didn't even know she was getting to the bulimia. She stood up and said, "Humor me a moment, okay? We're going to do a little experiment. Could you crawl under my desk please?"

I was like *What?* but she was smiling. "It's kind of a game. Just go with it."

So I got on my hands and knees and stuck my head and

shoulders in the nook where her legs usually went. "Okay," I said. "Am I looking for something?"

"No," her voice floated down to me. "But try to actually fit in there, all right?"

"Uh, okay." I had my doubts, but I jammed myself in. I had to hug my knees to my chest and keep my head sideways on my knees. There was no way to relax.

Then, to make it more bizarre, Dr. Giulia said, "Excellent. Now I'm going to try to fit my chair in place, okay?"

Was she nuts? There was no way! The chair pressed against me. A cramp started in my hamstring. My neck ached.

"Comfortable?" she called.

"Uh…no. Not at all." I wasn't laughing anymore. It was obvious I didn't fit.

She pulled the chair away and crouched down to look at me. "Really?" she said. She asked it sincerely too. "You don't like this?"

"No. Can I come out now?"

"Of course you can." She gave me a hand up.

As we stood there, looking down at the space, she said, "That's the prison you made for yourself with bulimia. Trying to fit yourself into a space that's too small."

I looked at the nook under her desk, then up at her face. I felt dizzy.

"But the most important thing is, you admitted you wanted to come out."

Okay, okay, cheesy, I know, but it actually made me get teary-eyed.

"Your life has become reduced to this." She gestured to that tiny hole I'd crammed myself in. "You define yourself this way. Remember how you told me you hated it when your mom became a 'sick person'? How she became to everyone 'a woman with cancer' instead of interesting, talented Annabeth, your mom? Well, the same thing has happened to you, but you're doing it to yourself. Your world has gotten so small with all you've given up to do this."

She had Aunt Izzy and I make a pact of total honesty before we left the country. I couldn't lie or hide a binge if one happened. Or, rather, *when* one happened. She assured me they *would* happen, and that I was to "treat myself with compassion" when they did. My binges, she said, were "a substitute for confronting painful feelings," just like my dad's drinking. Both my dad and I had to work to find healthier ways to deal.

Deal with *what* I wanted to know. Why was life so hard for me? Why was I such a baby? I didn't know, but in our pact of honesty, I promised to let Aunt Izzy know when I wanted to binge and she would help divert me. I was supposed to go do something else really active, like run. I couldn't imagine being able to divert a binge once one took hold of me—it felt like being possessed—but I said I was ready to try. Heck, I'd do just about anything to get rid of the DRH.

What's DRH? My Disgusting, Repulsive Habit. No more SR, because it's no longer secret, *and* it's not a remedy for anything.

So, sure, I'd try to divert a binge.

Fortunately for me, Ghana turned out to be quite the diversion.

★★★

Once Aunt Izzy woke up, it was nothing but *go go go*. She and her crew had already been over here five different times, beginning three years ago. That day, they were visiting an orphanage in Kumasi to do some follow-up. We weren't going to spend a lot of time in Kumasi; the heart of the documentary was a group of orphans in a smaller village called Tafi Atome (pronounced like Taffy Ah-TOE-may).

Aunt Izzy's crew was small on this trip. She had a bigger team back home for editing and production, but here, she'd brought just three other people and they had the weirdest collection of names. Pearl Hays was her main assistant and a camera person. Just like her name, everything about her was round and pale. Wide in the hips, well-endowed in the boob department, with a natural sway when she walked, she wore her almost-white blond hair in a thick braid down her back. She was a big woman, fat by L.A. standards, but she knew how to dress for her size, and she never apologized. She could laugh louder than anyone I'd ever met.

Dimple Singh—is that the coolest name or what?—was a skinny Indian woman who did sound production. Everything about her was straight and flat compared to Pearl. She kept her hair cut short, which made her dark eyes stand out even more.

The cinematographer was the only man on the trip and won the prize for the absolute best name. Kick McKew was originally from West Virginia. His funny expressions and his soft hill accent always made me grin—like, when we stepped out of the compound of our hotel, lugging equipment to Ben's van, Kick said, "Whew. It's hotter than the hinges of hell."

He was right. The heavy air pulled on my limbs as I moved through it.

Once in the van, crawling through snarled, chaotic traffic, Kick announced, "Well, we're off like a herd of turtles."

I glued myself to the van windows, leaving nose prints I'm sure.

Women (and some men) carried outrageous things on their *heads*—loads of firewood, flats of sunglasses, a tall stack of pillows, metal tubs piled with plastic bags of water (that the entire team and Ben made of point of telling me *never* to drink). These people talked, walked, and gestured without their loads ever losing balance.

Traffic careened along, sometimes five vehicles competed with each other across what looked like three lanes, with plenty of bicycles and motor scooters whizzing between them too.

At every intersection people walked between the rows of cars selling maps, toothbrushes, dried plantain chips, peanuts, pastries, and cassettes.

The heat wrapped itself around me, giving me the woozy sensation of an out-of-body experience. The smells were so intense, the sun so piercingly bright, the sounds so jarring.

A girl my age rapped on the side of the van, thrusting her open hand through my window. "Please. Please," she said. The entire right side of her head was blistered from a burn, with actual bubbles in the skin. Her right eye was gone, the lid pulled taut so that only a small slit of emptiness showed above her stark cheekbone.

Thank God I was sitting down, because my legs went totally weak. I felt all my joints and limbs just disconnect from my body, like the slightest breeze (not that there was much chance of one of those!) would detach them and they'd blow away.

The van began to pull forward. "Wait!" I cried, digging in my pockets. I handed the girl a fistful of the bright, fake-looking money I'd exchanged at the airport the night before.

"Whoa, Hannah, that's a lot," Kick said.

But I placed the money in the girl's hands. Her skin was remarkably cool in this heat.

"*Medasi, medasi,*" she chanted as we pulled away. *Thank you.*

"You okay?" Aunt Izzy asked me, looking back from her shotgun seat next to Ben.

I nodded, but the image of the girl's face was permanently seared on my brain.

We finally got out of Accra, heading north for Kumasi, farther into Ghana, farther from my life. I didn't know if that was a good or bad thing, getting farther from my life. My life was pretty sucky, but at least I *knew* it. Every single thing I laid my eyes on here was strange and unfamiliar to me.

A young girl walked with a wooden tray of shiny red tomatoes balanced perfectly on her head. I wondered if she had friends she trusted. Did she wonder *Am I pretty enough? Thin enough?*

★☆★

In Kumasi, people surrounded our van like my parents were on board. It had been a while since I'd experienced this kind of fanfare, and it had never before been directed at *me*. Little kids ran up to touch me then ran away. Everyone called out *"Obruni!"* to us: *"Obruni,* hello!"

Obruni means white person. I'm not sure what language it is, since there isn't one official language in Ghana. Even a little boy in his mother's arms cried out the greeting like a kid might say, "Santa Claus!" It was kind of funny, but also incredibly weird. I mean, I can't imagine calling out, "Hello, black person!" when I saw one at home.

While Aunt Izzy and her team unloaded equipment onto the sidewalk at the orphanage, children tugged on me, asked me my name, wanted me to take their pictures, wanted to touch my skin and hair. When someone patted my butt, I wheeled around, but it was just a little boy, maybe five years old. He then patted his own butt as if he was trying to see if I felt like he did. Thick heavy traffic crawled past us, everyone looking to see what the commotion was.

"Sister, sister," one man in a car sang at Pearl, leaning out his window. He didn't call like to get her attention; he said it more in an admiring tone, the way someone at a museum might look at *Starry Night* and say, "Van Gogh, Van Gogh."

Pearl smirked a bit but tossed her braid as she hefted camera equipment in the brigade from van to orphanage door. I could tell she was trying not to laugh.

The man, stuck in traffic, raised his voice. "Oh, please, Miss Fatty. Give me one look."

I gasped. How rude. "What a jerk," I said.

But Pearl laughed. "It's a compliment, sweetie. Calling me 'fatty' is the same as someone whistling back home."

I looked at Ben, who nodded. I also noticed he looked at Pearl with appreciation.

"Ghana is good for my ego," Pearl said.

Children surrounded me, pressed their hands on me, asking if they could have my camera, my watch, my shoes. My claustrophobia tipped toward meltdown.

I ran into the orphanage, after the team, afraid to be left in the crowd alone.

Inside, I couldn't shake the dream-like blur. Constant noise, chaos, like I was getting live streaming video from about fifty different sources. The heat pressed me down.

Aunt Izzy's team filmed and interviewed orphans while I hovered and watched. Their stories made me feel that limbs-might-detach sensation again.

★ ✫ ★

During a break, Kick said, "Maybe our scope is too broad. We could do a whole series on Darfur alone."

"Or Sierra Leone," Dimple said.

"Or Congo or Rwanda or Zimbabwe," Aunt Izzy said, eyes blazing. "But that's the *point*. This whole *continent* is turning into a land of orphans! I want to do *that* story. The bigger story."

Next, they talked to children who looked like the ones in the geography film, who had hands, arms, or eyes missing. Their stories made my skin buzz. I listened to four of these interviews before I began to fantasize about a binge. I had three pastries from the hotel wrapped in napkins at the bottom of my backpack, along with a Luna bar.

After three more interviews, the buzzing was just too much. Sweating, woozy, and leveled, I went in search of a bathroom.

When I found it, I stood on the slanted stone floor, listening to flies buzz in the rough troughs. No door, no water, no toilet paper.

A binge and purge in Africa was going to be very hard to pull off.

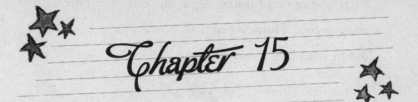

Chapter 15

115. Being safe

116. Having a home

117. Never having been physically harmed by anyone

118. Having my entire body intact

That night, in a new hotel room, sharing a double bed with Aunt Izzy, I couldn't sleep.

I realized I'd gone four days without a binge or purge. Was I fatter? The hotel's room didn't have a mirror, so I couldn't even look at myself.

Trying hard not to jostle the bed and wake Aunt Izzy, I reached down for my duffel bag. In the dark, I groped around until I felt my mother's pink cashmere sweater. I pulled it up to my cheek and breathed deep. Even with the ever present smells of Africa all around me—palm oil and smoke—there she was. The lemon scent of my mother.

What was my dad doing right this minute? Thinking of my mother too? Thinking of me?

Did he miss me? I missed him.

★☆★

We began our long drive to Tafi Atome in the morning. We stopped, hours later, for lunch, where I ate red-red—a stew made from cowpeas (what they call black-eyed peas) with red palm oil, tomatoes, *really* hot peppers, and onion.

Market stalls surrounded the roadside café—pyramids of oranges and coconuts, hills of limes, plastic flip-flops, used empty cans, rabbits strung up by their feet, chickens hanging in bouquets of three, whole goats, goat heads, goat legs, a pig.

I even saw a stall selling ingredients to make voodoo fetishes. Ben explained that Vodun is a real religion, but the idea we have in our heads of voodoo dolls and witch doctors all came from Western movies. I was already heat-dazed, my senses stupefied, as I gawked at buckets of vulture heads, monkey paws, monkey *testicles*, parrot wings, and dried chameleons. Coiled dead snakes, tongues of who knows what, horns, bats. Hooves, quills, a cheetah skin.

I watched people bargain over these items—the lemons, the tin cans, the dog heads—an aggressive process with lots of huffing, high-pitched cries of indignation, and people storming away from each other only to be called back. It made me afraid to buy anything.

I saw shiny bead necklaces I wanted to buy—not to wear but to disassemble for my cities. The bright colors tugged on me. I heard my mother's voice say, "Our Hannah is a magpie."

An African man saw me looking and said, "Ah, sister likes the beads, yes?" He tried to draw me closer, but my heart pounded and I scurried back to my aunt. The bargaining stressed me out. Why couldn't there just be a fixed price?

"Sss! Sss!" a woman hissed at me—when a Ghanaian wants your attention, they hiss, kind of like we do to shush someone, but just an *s*, not an *sh*. "You like the beads? Mine are better. See."

I was so relieved to drive away from all that wheeling and wheedling and demanding.

As we pulled away, I caught a last, longing glimpse of the beads as they flashed in the sun.

★☆★

Later that day, after the highways turned into red dirt roads, we finally reached Tafi Atome.

The village—only the size of a football field—sat plunked down in the middle of the rain forest, nothing more than two main dirt streets with three shops, a visitor's center, and one restaurant. The school was the biggest and best structure, and the village water pump—in the schoolyard—marked the center of the village. Residential homes stood on the outside edge of the two main streets; smaller roads lined with houses disappeared into the jungle.

As Ben parked in the schoolyard, he honked the horn, and people came running from all directions. The villagers and the film team greeted each other by name.

The second I stepped out of the van, a monkey snatched the sunglasses off the top of my head (and a few strands of hair with it)!

Villagers and the film crew laughed as I turned red with anger.

The village had created a sanctuary to protect the Mona monkeys that lived there. You could've fooled me that the Mona monkeys were endangered; the little brats were everywhere. Small and dark—the size of house cats—with white faces and bellies, and long tails, they leapt onto roofs and branches of trees, playing, wrestling, tumbling with each other.

I watched my favorite pair of sunglasses go from tin roof to tin roof and then into the dense trees. Izzy shrugged at me.

I tried to let it go when Modesta, one of the main subjects of the documentary, approached the van. Aunt Izzy had followed her for three years now. I felt like I already knew her, I'd watched so much footage of her already—a leggy dark black twig with luxuriant lashes any movie star would envy framing her enormous eyes. She wore an oilcloth print wrapped around herself, tied at one bony shoulder. Her smile was million-watt when directed at my aunt.

They hugged each other.

When Aunt Izzy introduced me to Modesta, Modesta's beam vanished. She nodded and looked at the ground.

"Why don't you show Hannah the house?" Aunt Izzy asked.

Modesta turned and walked into the house. I had to run to follow her.

I'd already seen some of this house—a cinder block building painted bright blue with salmon trim—in the footage from previous trips. What made Tafi Atome special compared to the other villages was that they'd given an entire house to the orphans who could not be absorbed into relatives' homes. Eleven orphans lived there—a big number when you considered the small size of the village. All the orphans attended school. Everyone in the village pitched in for their clothing and food. Modesta was the oldest, so she looked after the smaller ones.

She walked through the house, not really explaining anything, hardly looking at me. Great. I had to travel half a world away for another girl not to like me?

The small rooms inside were lined with cots, some bed rolls on the packed dirt floors. Although the beds' blankets were threadbare in places, each bed had been neatly made. "It's really very nice," I said, trying to get her to show me a hint of friendliness.

She nodded.

I didn't notice a bathroom, but I found out later that none of the houses in Tafi Atome had running water. I looked around, noting the absence of outlets and light switches.

Back outside, on the porch, Modesta crossed her arms over her flat chest and looked out at Kick and Dimple playing football—what we call soccer—with several of the children. More than eleven kids were playing, so I didn't know how to tell the orphans from the kids with parents.

The van was gone. I wondered where Ben had gone.

My stomach growled.

I clamped a hand over my belly. "The lion wants his dinner?" Modesta asked.

I laughed. She didn't even crack a smile.

It struck me that I hadn't felt *hungry* in a long, long time.

I felt *good*.

I didn't have a headache or that awful hangover feeling. I wasn't tired.

This was all new.

Aunt Izzy and Pearl came up on the porch to talk to Modesta, other children following them. I sat down on the wide concrete edge, wondering why Modesta didn't like me.

I was surprised Izzy and Pearl didn't film. They seemed content to hang out and chat with children on their laps. When Dimple grew tired of the football game, she joined us too. The kids asked us questions, about the U.S., about Ohio, about our politics, about California.

"California?" a young boy named Rafael asked, pronouncing all five syllables. "Do you know any movie stars?"

I froze.

I couldn't make eye contact with any of the film team. *Don't give me away. Don't give me away,* I begged in my head.

"There are movie stars everywhere in Los Angeles," I said. "You get used to it. They're just regular people."

"You are so lucky," Rafael said. "I would like to meet Will Smith. Or Matt Damon. Or Caleb Carlisle."

How did Rafael know these names? Where was the closest movie theater to Tafi Atome?

"You are so lucky," Rafael repeated. "Tell me the movie stars you have met."

Dimple took out a small recorder, which distracted him. The kids sang songs for us, then laughed when Dimple played their own voices back.

It grew dark, and I did everything I could to suppress the snarling noises in my belly, keeping my arms pressed hard across it. Parents began to steal up to the porch and, with gentle whispers, summon their children home for dinner. The cook fires and delicious aromas wafting through the dark violet sky tortured me and my empty stomach.

I recognized our van's puttering noise approaching through the darkness. The children remaining on the porch all cheered, and I realized our team was feeding the orphans tonight.

Ben and one of the older orphans—a tall, serious young man named Philomel—emerged from the van and carried cardboard boxes up to the porch. Everyone got a "tray" of newspaper holding rice, fish, and fried yams, all covered in a spicy tomato sauce.

I couldn't remember the last time food had tasted so good. I remembered Izzy's advice to savor each bite, to truly taste each flavor. I wanted to scarf down the entire tray, but recognized I was full when there was still plenty left. Rafael and the others devoured my leftovers.

Modesta and Philomel made the children wash their hands and faces after the meal, and as they came scampering back from the pump one by one, I saw them going through our trash bag, taking empty water bottles and an empty film canister.

After dinner, we walked to the visitor's center, where it seemed the entire village had gathered for drumming and dancing. I still couldn't get a smile from Modesta, but Rafael carried my white plastic chair for me on his head. He balanced it there with one hand and took me by the hand with his other, leading me to the drum circle. A Dutch couple was there—they were staying in someone's guest room—and a German college student who had paid to camp in the yard of the visitor's center. And us.

We set up chairs in an aerobic circle around an eye-stinging fire, and the men—including tall, serious Philomel—played huge, chest-high drums.

The women and children danced in a circle around the drummers. Most of the women were draped in brightly colored oilcloth. They became a kaleidoscope to my travel-bleary eyes as they jumped, turned, and twisted in the dusty circle, their skin glistening.

One woman danced with a baby wrapped to her back. I watched in amazement as the baby never stirred or cried through the bouncing, jostling, and noise.

Dancers gestured for us to join them. The Dutch couple and the German student jumped right up. So did Pearl and Aunt Izzy. I scooched down in my chair and tried to be invisible.

The weird thing was, the music made me *want* to dance. I wanted to move after spending most of the day in the van. But…but what? It had become my habit to hold back? To be chicken? To worry about what others might think?

I watched the Dutch couple. They looked silly. But did anyone care? Was anyone mocking them? Of course not. All the faces smiled, white teeth flashing through the dark.

I thought of those beads I'd seen at lunch.

Because of those beads, I let two village girls pull me into the circle.

They shouted their names over the music. One was Ekuba. Her friend was Beauty. Had I heard that right over the music? Beauty would be mocked back home for her wide hips and the rolls around her middle, but she really *was* beautiful, I thought, with her dimples, her long lashes, her sweet smile.

The music was wild—the drums like your own pulse amplified. I watched Ekuba and Beauty trying to copy their steps and turns. I actually got into a groove and felt I had a rhythm. I lost myself. I found my trance. Just like with my DRH.

Only I didn't feel nothing.

I felt something better: I felt joy. I felt life. I felt happy.

Modesta's gaze met mine, briefly, and I thought she might smile, but she whirled away.

When the music stopped, I dripped with grimy sweat. I *stunk*, but since I could also smell every other living being in the immediate vicinity, I didn't figure it mattered. I stepped outside the circle of chairs to catch my breath as the drummers began pounding out the next song.

In the dark, away from the heat of the fires, smaller kids played hide-and-seek on the outskirts of the circle. One used me to hide from the others.

I looked up at the purple sky. "I am in *Africa*," I whispered.

A goat brushed by me.

"I am *dancing* in Africa, in the middle of the night, in the middle of a village, in the middle of the jungle."

There was a reason to be happy if ever I'd had one.

I vowed to be braver. To *do* the very next thing that scared me.

Eventually, the drumming ended.

Rafael materialized from the darkness, my chair on his head, and took my hand again. I tripped over a goat and her kids in the shadows, nearly falling. The goat baaed at me.

Modesta's voice came through the darkness. "Sister goat says cross words to you."

The children giggled.

Rafael led me and the rest of the team back to the van. Izzy began explaining where everyone was staying. We'd be in private residences, with people who'd volunteered to host us. Izzy and I would stay with one of the schoolteachers.

"Han-nah can stay with us," Modesta said. She made my name rhyme with Ghana.

Izzy raised her eyebrows at me. She wasn't going to leave me if I didn't want it.

I had just vowed to do the very next thing that scared me.

I watched myself, as if from far away, open my mouth and say, "I'd love to stay here."

Modesta smiled. *Finally.* She smiled at *me.*

I hefted my duffel bag to my shoulder, hugged Aunt Izzy good night, and followed Modesta.

I was tired in that really exquisite way, like when you've spent the whole day hiking or at an amusement park. I craved one of those tidy little cots. I wanted to sink into delicious sleep.

But my favorite African day was topped by my worst night.

Chapter 16

By this point, I was so drained I could hardly stand. I pictured myself falling to sleep on one of the mats on the floor, but Modesta led me around to the back of the house and opened a door into a room with one bed.

She'd prepared a private room for me. That was an honor. "Oh, Modesta. I-I don't mind sleeping with everyone else."

She frowned. "This room is not satisfactory?"

"Oh yes! It is. It's wonderful!" I tripped all over myself not to offend her. "Thank you."

She nodded. "Good night," she said, and slipped away into the darkness.

This private room had an outside entrance. I fumbled in my duffel bag for my flashlight. I shone it around the room's concrete walls. No door connected the room to the rest of the house. I stood in the open doorway and turned my light toward the trees. I *had* to pee. There's *no way* I could hold it until morning. Just my luck, the orphan's house had to be on the outskirts of town, with the toilet even deeper into the rain forest.

I'd vowed to do the very next thing that scared me. *But you already did*, a whiny little voice protested in my head.

I inched down the dark path, heart in my throat. The kids do this, I told myself. They come out here and do this all the time. It can't be *that* dangerous.

A shriek from the trees above whipped me around and my legs raced me back to the start of the path before I was even aware of moving. What *was* that? A bird? Some kind of panther? Did I even want to know? Forget it! Just forget it. I should pee right here, off the path. Who would even know? But when I shone my light at the side of the trail, assessing whether this was a safe place to crouch, I saw, climbing up a tree trunk, a spider *as big as my hand*.

I fled back to my room and slid the wooden latch into place, locking my door.

I inspected the room with my flashlight. There were three windows—no screens of course—and one small bed on a wooden platform. That was it.

Above the windows were thick cloths rolled up and tied that you could release to keep the bugs out. If I closed the drapes, the room would be sweltering. The mosquitoes didn't seem too bad, plus I was taking malaria pills…but…but…I thought of that monstrous spider.

I'd never be able to sleep as long as I thought that CD-sized spider could crawl into my room!

I released the strings to unfurl the makeshift drapes.

Within seconds, the room became a sauna.

I eyed the bed's legs. In the inch or two visible before the oilcloth drape covered them, I saw the barbed wire wrapped around the legs—to keep snakes from climbing into bed with me.

I stripped down and used baby wipes and a bottle of water to mop most of the sweat, smoke, and red dust from my skin. I stuffed the dirty baby wipes into a plastic grocery bag. (I'd learned not to throw anything away. You never knew when it could be useful.) A clean T-shirt and shorts made me feel a little better.

But I still had to pee.

Bad.

I felt so far from home, so afraid, so alone. I wanted my mother.

I wanted my father. I wanted him to be healthy and normal, so he could be my dad again and I wouldn't be standing here half a world away too exhausted to stand but about to pee my pants.

What if I just peed right outside my door? No, no, no, if Modesta or anyone saw me it would be unforgivably rude.

Hey…I eyed the plastic bag already full of baby wipes. Why not? Wouldn't the wipes absorb it? Desperate times called for desperate measures. I'd done worse in my life after all.

It worked pretty well, actually, and it was one of those blessed, wonderful I've-held-it-too-long pees that felt so *amazingly* good I wanted to put it on my reasons to be happy list! Ahh…

I tied the bag, knotting it tight. I'd be sure to get it to the trash in the morning.

Feeling giddy with relief, I pulled back the mosquito netting on the bed. The weariness clung deep down in my bones. Sleep was going to be sweet indeed.

The bed was on the small side. To remain under the mosquito net, I couldn't extend my legs. Oh well. I laid on my back, knees bent, arms crossed over my chest, clutching my flashlight. I turned the flashlight off. I was so tired, I could have slept in a back bend if I had to.

I closed my eyes.

Sweat trickled through my hair.

The air seemed to simmer. And it was suddenly so *noisy*.

An entire universe of insects conducted a symphony outside, chirping, whirring, droning.

The whole forest come alive with drips, creaks, cracks, and rattles.

Another of those piercing shrieks.

I am never going to sleep.

But, apparently, I did.

I know I slept because a hideous heart-in-your-mouth noise yanked me awake.

A goat.

A goat that sounded like he had a microphone and was *in my room!* I swear. I turned on my flashlight and shone it around the room.

He baaed again.

Oh.

My.

God.

He was so *loud*. He must be *right outside* one of my windows!

I turned off my flashlight and pretzled my sweaty self back into my contorted position.

The goat continued yelling. *Another* goat, somewhere else in the village, began to answer.

They had quite the heated, insistent conversation. I checked the room *again* with a flashlight because I *swore* the one goat sounded like he was there, *right next to me*. If the floor hadn't been dirt I would've bet a million dollars that he was directly under the house.

The goats continued their debate for forty minutes. I timed them. Somehow, miraculously, I got used to them, or was completely drained enough to drift off to damp, stinky sleep…

I woke with a shriek when the *bed moved beneath me*. I dropped my flashlight and then scrambled in panic, hands fumbling over the sheets to find it, hoping not to land on anything unexpected. The bed moved again—creaking and moving side to side—as something bumped it from underneath. *Something was in here! Something was in the room with me!* I found the flashlight and stood on the bed, draped in netting, turning the light on in time to see a black-and-white goat crawl on his knees out from under the oilcloth drape.

The goat *was* in the room with me. There'd been a goat under my bed!

He clicked to the door on his cloven hooves, then bleated again.

The goat butted the door with his curled horns as if to make the point, clear as any house-trained dog, that he wanted *out*, thank you very much.

I collapsed cross-legged on the bed, one hand on my heart.

He *kept* yelling. How could anyone else in the house sleep? Why didn't Modesta come running at the sound of him banging his head on the door?

Finally, exasperated, not knowing what else to do, I opened the door and let the goat out. He trotted away into the rainy darkness.

I locked the door and checked under the bed for any other surprises (there were none). As soon as I'd crawled back into bed, another one of those blood-curdling screams came from the jungle. Oh no! Great. Just great. Had I just allowed one of the orphans' goats to be slaughtered by wild animals? Modesta would really love me now.

I obsessed over that little goat, certain I'd find its mutilated body in the dawn's early light.

Somehow, from utter exhaustion, I dissolved into sleep again. My dreams were full of bloody goat heads.

BANG!

I was on my feet, wrapped in mosquito netting, flashlight on.
BANG!

Over my head. The ceiling was falling in! I pictured some huge creature tearing the roof off, trying to kill me.

BANG, BANG, BANG! Then several lesser taps, then a clatter.

Then a chatter. A *chi-chi-chi*, reminding me of a squirrel.

The monkeys.

The monkeys were on the roof.

I checked my watch. It was 4 a.m.

Feeling beat up, I crumpled yet again back on the bed (the netting such a giant mess there was no hope of me fixing it by myself), but the monkeys were just warming up. There may as well have been a troupe of tap dancers doing a recital above my head.

At 5 a.m., I gave up. I wiped my drenched self down again (didn't have to pee now, having sweated all liquid out of my body during the night) and dressed.

When I stepped outside, the fresh air felt like receiving a gift.

To my surprise, several people were already up and going about their business. Many women had cook fires going in their yards.

I found Aunt Izzy with Modesta and another girl out front, already tending to something cooking in a pot. Several red chickens and three goats wandered near them. I thought I identified my buddy—the one with black and white spots.

Aunt Izzy hugged me. "You weren't lonesome, were you?" she asked. "All alone?"

I burst out laughing, which made Modesta cock her close-cropped head at me. "Oh, I wasn't alone," I said. I gestured to the goats. "I hope it's all right that I let the goat out last night."

Modesta nodded, no apology, no explanation. Just a nod that said, *Of course. What a silly question.*

I couldn't stop giggling. My terror from last night seemed absurd now. I'd been petrified. But I'd done it. I'd done something scary, and I'd survived.

"Did you sleep well?" Modesta asked.

I thought again of my private room, of the other rooms lined with mattresses and beds, of the sacrifice and effort to give me such a gracious gift. "Very well," I lied. "Thank you so much."

She beamed at me, her somber face transformed.

"I am glad," she said. "You shall stay with us again."

There was nothing to say but "thank you."

We were distracted by Rafael and another boy emerging from my room with my tied-shut trash bag. "We will take away your trash for you, sister," Rafael announced, already beginning to untie the top of the bag. I remembered the children rooting through our trash the day before.

"No, no, that's all right!" I snatched the bag from him, my face red.

I guess I couldn't get too cocky about my newfound bravery. I was still too scared for them to discover my pee-soaked baby wipes.

Chapter 17

A week later, I stood at the village pump with a fuming Modesta. She waited for a late child to arrive for a bath (she'd already supervised the scrubbing of three others). I looked at Modesta's blazing eyes and felt bad for adorable Englebert, the guilty party.

She paced, barefooted, on the packed earth.

I flipped through the photos I'd taken on my digital camera. I'd also filmed a couple movies, and I played one back of Modesta leading the smaller children in a song with lots of clapping.

She shook her head when she heard her own voice. "Why would anyone care what I have to say?" I knew she was talking about Aunty Izzy's documentary, not my little film.

"Lots of people should," I said. "You're a strong, tough survivor."

"What else is there to do but survive?" she asked, her

question genuine. She slapped a towel over her shoulder and scowled down the street.

Ekuba and Beauty strolled up to the pump to fill buckets with water. "Good morning, sister," we all said to each other.

The day before, Beauty had taught me how to feed mangos to the monkeys, much to the delight of the younger orphans. Beauty and Ekuba also brushed my hair and braided it with beads and tiny shells. I'm sure it looked ridiculous—Modesta had laughed out loud when she'd seen it.

When the girls carried their water away, Modesta resumed her pacing. "I will have to go get that boy myself. He never minds!"

"Give him five more minutes," I said. "It's a nice morning. Where else do we have to be?"

Modesta cocked her head at me, pretending to be annoyed, but she couldn't help lifting her face to the sun and smiling.

I continued flipping through my photos. I had several I was proud of, several that Aunt Izzy had asked permission to use. She'd even had me record with a real film camera a few times.

I came across my favorite candid picture of Modesta. She crouched, bare feet flat on the ground, knees up by her ears in her flexible Gumby-like way. Her left elbow was on her left knee but her hand rose to her face, her cheek leaning into her open palm.

Her skin, short burgundy hair, and muted purple dress

blended into the shadowy dusk behind her, so her huge, haunting eyes leapt out of the photo, the brightest visual in the shot.

I thought she was stunning in this picture, so thin, angular, and flexible. Her mind clearly elsewhere, she looked unveiled, her face so open.

"I love this picture of you," I said. "I'm going to print this one and keep it. I'll send you one."

She came close to me to look. When she saw it, she wrinkled her nose.

"Ach," she said, holding up a hand as if to shield her view. "That is a horrible picture!"

"What? You're kidding, right? You look like a supermodel!"

She made a face like she would spit.

"Modesta, are you serious? What's wrong with this picture? You look gorgeous."

She barked a harsh laugh. "I am too scrawny, too weak. My legs and arms look like that pile of sticks there." She pointed to a bundle of kindling.

"Modesta, you're *lean*, not weak. You look fit and strong."

She eyed me, lips pursed. "No, fit and strong is like *you*." She gestured to my legs. "I want legs like yours."

It was my turn to wrinkle my nose. "I'm fat, Modesta. You don't want my fat butt."

She whooped with laughter, then her smile vanished and her cold, stern look returned. "Fat? Ha! You can't call yourself fat," she sounded almost scolding, as if I'd been bragging. "Now Beauty, *she* is fat. You are strong, though. Your...*butt* looks like you can run fast."

I nodded. "I am fast."

She shook her head, eyes twinkling as if amused. "Fat," she repeated. She snorted.

"Beauty is beautiful," I said, hating how corny it sounded but wanting to defend her.

Modesta nodded.

"But you just said she was fat."

Modesta's brow furrowed. "You make no sense, Hah-nah. She is beautiful *because* she is not a stick person like me."

Oh. So me saying I was fat out loud like that had sounded like I was being a diva, like I'd said "I'm gorgeous" or something.

I laughed.

"What is so funny now, crazy girl?" She put her hands on her hips and stared me down as if I were one of the young orphans.

"What's funny is I have no idea what is beautiful here."

She tilted her head.

"I mean it." I tried to think of how to explain. "At home, at least where I live, there's a 'look' everybody wants. I don't fit the look, so I always feel like I'm ugly."

At this, Modesta looked confused.

"But here," I said, "I don't know how anyone is 'supposed' to look. I don't know who's popular. I don't know anything except who is friendly and who's not."

I wished I could explain to Modesta that I was friends with her because I *wanted* to be, even though I had no way of knowing if she was an "acceptable" person to be friends with. Same with Beauty and Ekuba. I talked to them and hung out with them, but it had never occurred to me to take my cue from Modesta about them. Although I spent time with all of them, the three girls never hung out together that I saw. They were friendly to each other, but clearly not close friends. I, however, was friends with all three.

I didn't know who in the village was rich or poor, considered popular or undesirable, or if their clothes were fashionable or laughable. I didn't know what anyone's parents did. I couldn't even tell who was pretty or not. How strange that such wild, unfamiliar territory made it easier to find myself.

Slowly, I was rebuilding myself—as meticulously as one of my miniature cities.

"So," Modesta said as she looked down, tracing a circle in the red dirt with her toe, "in America, I would be beautiful?"

"Yes," I said. "But you're beautiful here too."

She waved her hand at me, dismissing this idea.

Then along came Englebert, the very boy she'd been waiting for.

"You are the laziest boy!" she said, smacking him on the side of his head, but only playfully. They both laughed.

"If I had to be bathed," Englebert protested, "I thought I should get dirty first."

He stripped down right there at the pump, as had the other three before him, two girls and one boy. Being nude was no big deal here. Everyone, even adults, could be seen naked, especially here at the pump or bathing on their porches. People just sudsed up with no screens or privacy. It had taken me a while to get used to that. No one, but me, looked twice at a naked person. It was actually kind of cool to see all the different kinds of bodies.

I was still too much of a novelty, with my white, white flesh, to bathe at the pump. I sometimes felt like the Pied Piper, the way the little ones followed me to touch my hair and skin.

When I took a bath, I carried a big bucket of water behind the outhouse—which I had even started visiting after dark—and washed myself there, naked except for my flip-flops. I ignored the giggles I heard from the woods. I knew the children laughed only at my freakish, ghostly skin, not my shape, or even at seeing my private parts. "I hear you," I'd call, shampooing my hair. More giggles, then the rustling of leaves as they ran away.

I hadn't binged or purged in over two weeks, mostly because it was too difficult there.

I felt *good*. I had energy. I felt rested. Awake. Curious.

Modesta scrubbed Englebert with a zeal that looked like it hurt. He took it like a trouper, his face stoic but his eyes bright.

At the end of the alley, Aunt Izzy appeared, talking to one of the village elders. She was simply talking, not filming, and the two stood at the intersection of roads in a deep conversation.

When Englebert was rinsed off and dried, he put his clothes back on and scampered away. Once he'd left, Modesta folded her towels and said, not making eye contact, "In America, are you…beautiful?"

All my good feelings ran away with the rivulets of water making pink puddles in the dust.

"Nope." I tried to make my voice light and casual. "In America, they like girls bone thin, like, you know, like Dimple, the Indian woman? The one who does sound for my aunt?" I gestured down the alley where Aunt Izzy stood talking to the elder.

"Huh," Modesta said, mulling this. She watched Izzy a moment. "Your legs and butt," she said with a sly grin, "belong to all the women of your family. Your aunt, she has them too."

"No, she doesn't!" I said. "Aunt Izzy is so thin and fit. Her legs are—"

I broke off and stared. She *did*. She *was* thin and fit, *and* she had big, well-muscled thighs and plenty of booty. How had I never noticed this before? I'd always pictured her body as perfect. I shook my head, angry at myself. Her body *was* perfect.

"The women of your family pass it down to you," Modesta said. "Did your mother have such strong legs too?"

The hot, dusty landscape wavered. *My mother*. My mother was gone. I closed my eyes, trying to picture my mother. "I-I-you know what? I think I have a picture I can show you!"

I scrolled through my photos. I'd never deleted my favorite photo of her from the camera's memory card, even though I'd downloaded it to my computer over a year ago.

When I found it, I stared at it a moment before I showed it to Modesta. My mother, leaving for an awards ceremony, walking to the limo. She wore a violet backless gown. She held my father's hand and they walked away from the camera, but I'd called to them and they'd looked over their shoulders at me. The photo offered a perfect view of my mother's behind.

Her ample, curvy behind.

Modesta leaned next to me to see it. "It is so," she said.

I had my mother's butt. No matter what I did, I couldn't change this. Why would I want to?

"You look so much like her!" Modesta said.

I bit my tongue before I could say *I do not.* "Really?" I said instead.

"Oh yes. If you had not told me, I would know at once she was your mother."

Maybe I hadn't been switched at birth?

"Your father is a handsome man. You favor him as well." Modesta kept looking from the photo to my face, nodding as if to affirm what she said.

I wanted to hug and kiss her!

The photo blurred before me. God, how I missed my mom. But how much I missed my *dad* slammed into me too. I pictured him in rehab. How was he doing? Did he think of me?

I felt like an idiot when I realized Modesta must miss her parents too. How self-absorbed I was! "Do you-do you have a picture of your parents?" I asked.

She blinked but otherwise showed no emotion. "Only here." She tapped her head.

"What did they look like?"

She smiled. "Tall and thin," she said, gesturing to herself. "My father, he was strong before..." She stopped a moment, gazing into the distance. "A big, strong man. He used to carry me on his shoulders. My mama was thin. Even when she was growing a baby, she was thin. Stick legs, like me. But she was admired for her eyes and her singing voice."

"I'm so sorry they're gone," I whispered.

She looked at me, almost irritated or angry, it seemed, then she sighed.

The monkeys rattled the leaves. After a pause, she said, "I will go to school, you know. To university. In Accra perhaps. I will be a doctor. I will stop this plague that stole my parents."

She wore that grim, determined expression again. I knew she would do this, in spite of all the difficulties and obstacles. I saw it in her face and posture that she would *find a way* no matter what. I saw this was her driving force, her obsession, just as mine had been my DRH.

It struck me how much effort, how much time, planning, and expense I'd invested into something so stupid and absurd.

Modesta closed her eyes and lifted her face to the sun again. "How do they like the boys?"

I frowned. "What?"

"You said in America, they like the girls skinny. How do they like the boys?" She was dead serious, interested.

"Um…" I thought of movie stars. I thought of my dad. And, I couldn't help it, I thought of Kevin. In spite of everything, Kevin was lovely to look at, the big jerk. "Not so skinny, more muscled. Blond is good. Blond and tan."

She tilted her elegant head. "I think you are thinking of a certain boy."

I shrugged but felt a blush bloom in my cheeks.

That smile started on Modesta's face, the one that totally transformed her face. She seemed to have two expressions: stone-faced or beaming. "Yes, I think I am right. What is the boy's name?"

"Kevin," I admitted.

"Ah ha!" She sounded as if she'd beat me at some game. "Tell me about Kevin."

I thought a minute. "He's really nice to *look* at, but…Kevin's kind of a jerk. He's mean. He was rude to me. He wanted… you know, he was all creepy and grabby with my body."

"You *like* this boy?" She added a new expression to her repertoire: horror.

"No. I mean…well, I *did*. At least I thought I did. I mean—I felt lucky that he liked me."

"*Why?*"

What was it about the African sunlight that made it so easy to tell the truth?

"*He* liked *me*," I said. "He was beautiful and popular, and I'm...not."

She studied me a moment. "Huh," she finally said.

I'd been mean too, all because Kevin liked me.

Modesta gathered up her folded towels and said, "My mother told me, 'Beauty will take you there, but character will bring you back.'"

I froze. "My-my mom used to say something like that. She said, 'Pretty is as pretty does.'"

Modesta thought a moment then nodded. "Exactly."

I took half of the towels from her arms and walked the dusty alley toward the house.

"Is there no boy that you truly like?" Modesta asked. "Someone who *does* pretty?"

Jasper flooded into my mind.

"Ah, I see from your face that you do. Why did you not tell me about this boy first?"

I smiled. "He's not popular but he's very kind. He's been very nice to me."

"Do you like him?"

I nodded.

"Why?"

Why? I thought about that. "He gets this wonderful look on his face when he's playing the piano. Like he's in another world. He's very smart…and curious. He's nice to everyone. He's—he's brave. And different. Unique. He doesn't care what anyone else thinks of him; he does what he wants to do. He has this yellow wedge in his eye that I can't stop looking at when I'm around him. And this very slow smile. And his hair—"

I stopped, realizing Modesta had disappeared from my side. I turned back to see her standing still in the road. Two brown goats trotted past us.

"You do not *like* this person, Hah-nah. You *love* this person!"

I almost dropped the towels.

She caught up to me and peered into my face. "You do. Does he know this?"

I shook my head.

"You waste your time on this Bad Kevin when this beautiful boy is there?"

I shrugged. "I'm a chicken, Modesta."

She pushed me in the shoulder. "You must be brave!"

"I-I can't. I—he knows this thing about me. This ugly awful secret."

Modesta stepped away from me, then eyed me up and down. "What secret?"

"It's too…It's gross."

She narrowed her eyes at me then shook herself. "It is not so. Whatever this secret is, your true character cannot be hidden."

I wasn't so sure. My true character had been stuffed in a drawer so long with my secret stash of food that I wasn't sure how to bring it back—at least, I didn't know how to bring it back at home, and I couldn't live here in Ghana forever.

"You must tell him."

I joked, to make it easier. "Well, I can't, can I? He's not here."

"Write it to him."

"I'll be home before a letter from here reaches him."

She made the same exasperated clucking sound she'd made over Englebert. "Email him!"

I blinked. Modesta knew about email? I looked at the buildings surrounding us, buildings with no plumbing and no electricity.

She shuffled her bundle of towels and soap under one arm and grabbed my hand with the other. "We have email at the school! Come!"

Chapter 18

Modesta led me by the hand, as if I were one of the small orphans. She took me into the school building, which was wide open—no locks because there were no doors—to one sole computer under a giant Tupperware tub on a metal desk. She directed me to the rickety chair at the desk, lifted the Tupperware, and turned the computer on.

I listened to the musical chord of it coming to life with disbelief. They didn't have plumbing, but they had the Internet?

"This is where I study medicine," she said, "so I can go to university."

The Internet connection was fast—wireless. Satellites were easier to install than phone lines through the rain forest.

When I accessed my account, I blinked, stunned. My inbox was full of emails from my dad. A quick scan showed me he'd emailed me *every day*. Often more than once.

My eyes stung. It was suddenly hard to swallow.

"He has already written you, this boy?" Modesta asked, looking at my face.

I shook my head. "No. No, my dad—"

She squeezed my shoulder. I scrolled through the dates and opened his first one: *I hope you have arrived safely, Hannah Banana. What a great adventure you're going to have. I miss you already. I love you, Dad.*

He *did* miss me.

The next one, and the next, all of them, ended with *I miss you so much. I love you.*

He wrote about rehab. *I'm doing well and learning a lot about myself. The work I need to do (on myself) is hard and humbling. I want to do it, but I hate admitting it's not going to be easy. Or quick. How are you doing with your bulimia?*

Wow. I wondered how hard it had been for him to type the word *bulimia*. He'd never said it aloud to me.

When I'd finished all of his emails, I realized Modesta had slipped away.

I haven't binged in two weeks now, which feels great, I wrote to Dad. *I have to admit I've wanted to, though, every single day, more than once. Sounds like we're both in the middle of hard lessons. Africa is…overwhelming, but in a good way. This is going to change me; I can feel it. I miss you so much. I love you, Dad.*

I moved all of Dad's messages into a "Saved" folder. I couldn't stand to delete any of them. All that remained in my inbox were three emails from Mrs. DeTello. Nobody else knew my email. I don't have a Facebook or anything like that. Those things are too…complicated when you have famous parents.

DeTello was just checking in with me, wishing me well. I filled her in on some of my adventures so far, shared with her some of my progress, then asked her for a favor. *I need to email Jasper Jones about something. Do you think you could ask him for his email address? I don't know it and I don't know how to get it from here.* I stared at the message a long time before I hit send. Did I really *want* to contact him? Why would he want to hear from me after what he'd seen? I groaned to remember; he'd seen me eating trash! Shoveling it into my mouth like some revolting animal. I put my head down on the desk.

"Hah-nah?" A voice behind me made me jump. I turned to see tall, handsome Philomel in the doorway. "Are you well?"

"Oh! Yes, thanks. I was just…waiting." I gestured to the computer.

"I am looking for Modesta. Have you seen her?"

"She was just here with me. I'm not sure where she went."

He slipped away as soundlessly as he'd come. I watched through the window as he walked his graceful way across the soccer field toward the orphan house.

Why hadn't I thought to ask Modesta if *she* had a particular boy in mind?

I didn't hear back from DeTello.

I thought I was being so cool and chill, waiting two whole agonizing hours to check the computer.

Nothing.

I kept calculating the time change and figuring out, "Okay, she's had Jasper in class already, so she could've asked him. She should have sent it to me by now." Can you say obsessive?

Humiliation hung hot and heavy on my legs, like I struggled through quicksand.

"He doesn't want to talk to me," I told Modesta, miserable. She put her hands on her bony hips and rolled her eyes.

"You don't understand," I said. "He saw me do something terrible! I bet the teacher asked him for the email and he said 'No way. I don't want to talk to her.' He's probably glad I'm gone. He hopes I never come back."

"Hah-nah, Hah-nah, you talk crazy."

"You don't know! I'm a horrible person and he'd delete any message I sent him."

"Stop. Just stop."

"I'm mortified I even asked my teacher to ask him. I should've known better."

"Hah-nah! Don't eat the monkey!"

I shut up. *What did she just say?*

She leaned toward me and repeated, "Slow. Down. Don't eat the monkey."

I watched her lips move, trying to decipher what she'd said. "What is *that* supposed to mean?"

Modesta laughed—a musical, rare sound. She slapped her knee. "It means *slow down* and get the facts. Don't make up this *kaka* in your head before you know the truth."

"What does that have to do with *eating monkeys?*"

She waved a hand at me as if impatient. "In Eastern Africa, they eat monkeys," she said, disdain clear in her voice. "A French family moved to Kenya and brought their pet monkey. Their Kenyan cook's brother came to visit when the French family was on a holiday. The cook's brother's wife caught the monkey and cooked it. They didn't know it was a pet."

Was I insane? What was she talking about? What a *horrible* story! "Why would they cook someone else's monkey, even if they thought it was for food?"

She sighed. "Don't eat the monkey until you *know*."

I burst out laughing at the absurdity. And I tried. I *really tried*. I did everything in my power not to eat the monkey while I checked email every half hour for the rest of the day.

When I was forced to give up and go to bed, I hardly slept, sweating and tossing in my tiny bed as horribly as I had that first night. In the morning, before I'd even bathed, I threw on shorts and a T-shirt and ran to the school in the early dawn light.

A message from DeTello popped up like salvation.

Jasper's email was *jazzpurr* which made me smile. My heart kicked against my ribs.

Okay. Okay. Now what? Don't be a chicken. What do you want to tell him? "*Hi, Jasper. Not sure if you want to talk to me, but I wanted to apologize for dropping off the face of the earth.*" I filled him in on where I was and what I was doing.

I really wanted to apologize for what he'd seen me doing in the cafeteria. I really wanted to explain *that*. But I didn't know how.

You were a good friend during some rough times, so I'm sorry I didn't say good-bye. Hope all is well in the cafeteria and with your music.

I reread it about a hundred times. What a lame note. Oh well. I hit send and immediately regretted it.

After I sent the message, I stretched, then went running. Running for real. Not running because I felt freaked and was trying to flee from my need to binge. I ran with a goal in mind, keeping track of it, timing myself, before the sun would make exertion impossible.

Modesta was right: my thighs and butt were shaped the way they were for a *reason*. They were strong. They were fast. I ran through the monkey sanctuary, on trails that went around the perimeter of the village.

"Are you all right?" Aunt Izzy asked me as I returned to the village pump, soaked with sweat and panting. "Why are you running?"

I looked at her concerned face. "Because it feels good," I said. "Because it makes me feel strong. Because I'm going to train and join the track team again."

She smiled. "Good. Those are all the right reasons."

I vowed that I would not check email obsessively like I had the day before.

I bathed.

I wrote in my purple notebook:

119. The sounds of the rain forest at night

120. Fresh, hot (from the sun) pineapple out of the shell

121. Friends you can trust

122. Children singing in another language

123. Doing something you haven't done in a really long time
     that you've really missed

I helped Modesta get the children dressed and off to school.

I watched Aunt Izzy and the team film for a while.

I lurked around the empty orphan house.

I tried to do some of my own homework.

Mid-morning, I finally went back to the school. Modesta, at her desk, saw me and lifted an eyebrow. She knew why I was there.

My heart clutched in my throat when I saw it. There it was, a message from him already. What if it said *Get lost, freak*?

I opened it. *Hannah! It was so cool to hear where you are. I was afraid you moved schools and I didn't want to lose touch with you.*

Really? He'd noticed I'd been gone? He'd noticed enough

to wonder where I was? He wanted to stay in touch with me? I touched my hot cheeks, knowing I was blushing.

I was really sorry to hear about your dad on the news. I hope he's okay and you are too. If the universe could cut somebody a break right about now, I'd cast my vote for Hannah Carlisle.

P.S. Why would I not want to talk to you?

P.P.S. I'm really sorry I freaked you out that last day in the cafeteria.

Freaked *me* out? I thought I'd freaked *him*. Or totally made him sick.

I thought I should wait to write him back. Not seem too eager. But what the heck? I didn't want to play games. I wanted to be honest.

Jasper, thanks for your message. I think the universe heard you and gave me a break. My dad is doing well in an in-patient rehab program and I'm doing better too. Ghana is beautiful. I'm trying to take it all in and not miss anything! I pictured the yellow triangle in his eye. His long hair hanging in his eyes. His piano music. I just kept typing. *Um, about that day in the cafeteria? There's no way you should be apologizing! I'm sorry you had to see that. I obviously have some issues I need to work on.*

I looked at what I typed. What was wrong with me? He didn't want to know this!

I'm surprised you'd want to talk to me after seeing something so disgusting.

Students got up from their desks for their lunch break. I shouldn't hog the computer.

Anyway, thanks again. Hannah.

I smiled at the screen like an idiot. I felt kind of light, kind of warm…it took me a few minutes to recognize *happiness.*

I slept well, dreaming about my mother. We walked on the beach, hand in hand.

When I rose just before sunrise, I stretched and ran again.

After I bathed, I went to check my email before the students arrived at school.

Messages from Dad. A message from Jasper.

Jasper wrote: *Good luck working on your "issue" as you call it. You also called it "disgusting," but issues are nothing but human. Who doesn't have issues? The look on your face that day was so sad and haunted, I hope you find a way to stop it. I'd hate for you to feel that way ever again. As for worrying that I'd never talk to you again, I don't think there's much of anything you could do to scare me away at this point.*

I hope you know how lucky you are to be in Ghana, getting to go to a place not many other Americans ever visit. I've always wanted to go to Africa—Ghana, Senegal, Egypt, Kenya. Please savor it for me. Soak it up like a sponge so you can give me every detail when you get back. Speaking of getting back...when do you?

I pressed a hand to my heart a moment. Then I started typing, typing faster than I'd ever typed before. I told Jasper all about the burned girl in the street that first day, the smells, how scary it was to bargain in the markets, the orphans with limbs missing in Kumasi.

This trip has put all my cowardly concerns in perspective.

Modesta tapped my shoulder. Children's voices surrounded me. School was about to start.

"You write to the pretty boy?" she asked.

I nodded, face flaming.

She clucked her tongue. "Aren't you glad you didn't eat that monkey?"

Yes, I was. Very glad indeed.

Even more so that evening when Jasper had already answered. *You don't strike me as a cowardly person, Hannah. It really surprised me that you described yourself that way.*

Although that made warmth roll through me, it also meant Jasper didn't know the real me. He'd caught a glimpse of her when he'd seen me wolfing down those grilled cheese sandwiches...but whatever. That's okay. Let him, let *someone*, think of me as brave.

189

What are you doing for your Make a Difference Project? I typed. *I can't figure out what to do for mine. I can't figure out what "world" I want to impact, like DeTello says.*

I could've sat there writing to him for hours, if Aunt Izzy hadn't come in and told me it was nearly midnight and I'd better get some rest if I wanted to go with her to the Bonwire kente village the next day.

Chapter 19

We left at a painful hour the next morning, so early I didn't have time to email Jasper. I *tried* not to obsess over it. I told myself it would give me something to look forward to all day.

Long before the sun even thought about rising, our film team piled into the van to head to Bonwire. They were going to interview an orphan from Tafi Atome who'd become an apprentice to a kente cloth weaver last year.

I slept most of the drive and was groggy when we arrived at the shop. The space was crowded for filming, so I stayed in the courtyard of the shop and watched three workers weaving. The courtyard rang with the *click-clack* of their wooden shuttles on the looms. They even used their *feet* to weave, as well as their hands. They wove narrow strips, about four inches wide and over five feet long. I caught myself already describing it to Jasper in my head.

One tiny, shriveled man with a buzz of white hair wove

a piece in brilliant purple and white that I loved, its design intricate and complicated, like my cities. I watched the old man complete the final strip of the purple piece he had been working on for four days, then bring out the other strips and begin to sew them together into one piece the size of a tablecloth.

I wandered into the shop, but couldn't find that purple and white design.

I looked through single strips of cloth. I found another one I liked—this one red and yellow, with a design that made me think of Jasper.

Should I buy Jasper a souvenir from Ghana? My stomach fluttered. Emailing him was one thing, but the thought of facing him after what he'd seen me do made me want to creep away and disappear into the rain forest. Besides, I watched people bargaining for kente cloth, that aggressive, insane ritual that made me want to hide.

Thinking of Jasper reminded me of that day, after the awful art class fiasco, when he'd said, "They don't have the power to stop me from doing what I want."

What did *I* want?

I walked back across the courtyard, heart pounding. When I reached him, the old man said, "You like this piece." It was not a question.

"I think it's the most beautiful piece in the whole shop. I'd like to buy it."

He looked at me, then looked at the finished cloth folded in his lap. "Sit," he said, gesturing for me to sit across from him. I did.

He looked at me as if expecting something. After a long pause, he leaned forward and said softly, "You must ask me my price."

Oh! So he was willing to sell it? I grinned. "Uh...okay. What is your price?"

Very formally he said, "700,000 cedis."

That's roughly $70. That was reasonable, I thought.

"Okay!" I unzipped the little purse I had slung across my chest.

But he raised his hand and made that *Sss!* noise.

"Sister, now you must tell me *your* price. What would you offer for this cloth?"

Oh God. Not this. Where was Ben, our guide? I looked around, but Ben was nowhere to be seen. I hated this bargaining. My shoulders slumped.

The old man laughed. "Sister, it is a game."

"But..." I took a deep breath.

"Do not be afraid," he said.

I looked up at him, startled. The man looked me in the

eye, and I swore he knew everything about me. I *was* afraid. I was afraid of everything. It had gotten so *boring*.

He leaned forward in his cross-legged position and whispered to me, as if we were onstage and the audience shouldn't hear, "Offer me half."

Half? For this piece he'd worked on for weeks? He nodded again, encouraging me.

I couldn't bring myself to offer only half, so I said, "400,000 cedis."

His sweet, encouraging face changed and his chest puffed out. "Oh no!" He shook his head, his eyes flashing. "This cloth could never leave for so little as that!"

Little? "But you *told* me—"

He leaned forward again and whispered, "Come, sister, you can learn the game."

Do not be afraid.

I braced my shoulders. "500,000 cedis," I said.

Again, he looked outraged. "This cloth would never leave for less than 600,000 cedis!"

I cocked my head. "*If* I pay 600,000, may I also have one of those?" I pointed to a strip hanging nearby.

He laughed and clapped. "Yes! *That* is how to play! Yes, yes!"

He stood and formally handed the purple cloth to me. I

formally handed over my money. Then, he took down the strip I had pointed to and gave it to me.

"Actually," I said, "there is another strip inside that I liked better. Could I have that instead?"

He threw back his white head and laughed as if I'd told the best joke he'd ever heard. He squeezed my shoulder. "Yes, sister, yes. You should always get what you want."

I went inside the shop and picked up the strip I'd thought of buying for Jasper.

When I thanked the old man, he bowed to me.

Back in the van, Aunt Izzy said, "Do you know that old man is the chief of Bonwire?"

"What old man?"

"The man who made your cloth."

I peered through the window. The old man stood in front of the shop. He waved to me.

I have kente cloth woven by the chief of Bonwire!

As we hit the rutted red dirt road again, I hugged my purple cloth and thought about the chief's words: *You should always get what you want.*

Did I even know what that was anymore?

We stopped at another village, Ahwiaa, on the way back to Tafi Atome and I got a brief reminder of what I did want.

In one shop, the floor was tiled like mosaic, with broken china pieces. I was flooded with the wish to make one of my cities. I wanted to be crouching, hands in the dirt, with lots of little pieces of bright, gaudy material to work with. "This is beautiful," I said, pointing to the floor. The shopkeeper looked at me like I was insane for praising the floor instead of his wood carvings.

He shooed two red hens out of the way and tried to entice me toward his carvings—and *that's* when I saw the necklaces.

The necklaces were bright, strung with the most colorful, vivid beads I'd ever seen.

"Ah, sister likes the beads," the shopkeeper said, seeing the change come over my face.

The beads pulled me to them. Some, tiny as poppy seeds, were painted. Green with yellow stripes, red with green and yellow stripes, the most perfect robin's egg blue, cobalt.

I selected ten necklaces—that I planned to unstring—and a bulging bag of individual beads. I loved plunging my hand into the bowl of beads the shopkeeper showed me. How long had it been since I'd finished one of my cities? I'd started that one for my mom, but hadn't finished.

I threw back my shoulders and did the bargaining myself.

When we returned to Tafi Atome, the sun had begun to set, the sky that bloody red. I stretched and then ran the perimeter of the monkey sanctuary.

Sanctuary.

Running was my sanctuary. Running was the one place where I found the old Hannah still strong, still real, still beautiful.

I thought about what Jasper said—*You don't strike me as a cowardly person*—how I'd mistakenly thought that meant he didn't know me. Actually, the truth was the opposite. If he thought I was brave, then he knew the *real* me. He'd been able to see her, even when I couldn't see her myself.

Running, I saw her again.

She'd been there all along. I'd just forgotten where to find her.

Chapter 20

124. Having more than you need
125. Seeing an elephant (not in a zoo)
126. Drum music
127. Weaver birds
128. That mouthwatering, stomach-growling aroma of grilling meat

Running wasn't the only thing I returned to. I craved my art; I craved my cities. Each evening, I brought out the beads I'd bought in woodcarver's village and spread them on my bed, examining them by flashlight. I collected shells, strange nuts, and pebbles. I also collected these great brass figures that Philomel made.

Philomel had been trained in this way cool art called the "lost wax technique." He carved a figure out of wax— usually a traditional figure that had a proverb that went with it—then shaped a coal-clay ball around the wax figure. He'd bake the coal ball hard as cement, then nail a hole in the bottom of the ball so the melted wax ran out, turning the ball into a mold. Then he poured molten brass through the hole into the mold. He'd let it set several days before cracking the clay to release the tiny, shimmering brass crocodiles, turtles, birds, and abstract symbols. I ran my hands through clattering piles of them and *longed* to build one of my cities. I envisioned re-creating an African market in miniature form.

One day, the village of Tafi Atome had a feast. For some reason I never quite grasped, someone slaughtered a goat, roasted it, then made a fantastic groundnut soup with goat in it for the whole village to enjoy. The roasting meat smelled *divine*, and even Dimple—a vegetarian—closed her eyes and moaned appreciation at the aroma. When I asked her if she was going to eat some, she shrugged and said, "Of course. Being vegetarian here feels a little harsh and indulgent. I would never, ever refuse what they offered me."

The feast turned into a village party. Everyone pitched in and made whatever they could to share. I helped Modesta fry plantains, one of my favorite treats.

Everyone cheered when someone arrived in a big green van with lots of warm beer. When the soup was ready, people brought benches and chairs from their homes and we all ate, balancing bowls and plates in our laps, in the schoolyard.

The goat stew was really good. I mean *really*. For the first time in ages—what? almost a month?—I ate until I was full.

Full. The feeling upset me. The uncomfortable, stuffed sensation reminded me of a binge, although I hadn't *meant* to binge. I stopped eating, giving what was left in my bowl to little Englebert. I pressed a hand to my stomach and tried to shrug the new tension out of my shoulders.

Wouldn't it feel good?

No. No, no, no. Stop it.

You haven't done it in so long. What harm would it do just every now and then?

No, no.

I turned to Englebert, quelling the panic inside me. I noticed a brass lion hanging around his neck on a black string. "Did Philomel make that?" I asked.

He nodded.

"He's really good," I said.

"Thank you, Hah-nah," Philomel said, from a few chairs over.

"I really like them," I said. "I want to buy some."

Philomel, never one to miss a sale, pulled a clinking bundle from under his chair. As drumming and dancing began, he brought the bundle to my chair and opened the cloth on the dusty red ground, revealing hundreds of the tiny brass figures inside. I loved them even more, out here sparkling in the sun. They'd be so, so perfect to incorporate into my cities.

Modesta stirred what was left of the stew, watching us.

"Which one would you like to buy?" Philomel asked.

"All of them."

I thought his eyes would leap out of his face. I'm sure he thought I'd revealed myself to be a millionaire. I could've bought his entire stock for the equivalent of fifty dollars.

"I love them. I want them to—" How did I explain the cities? "I'd like to use them in some art I make."

"They are not just to look at," Philomel said. The crocodile I held, for instance, he told me represented adaptability. The turtle stood for a secure home. A beautiful piece of four curls coming together was the ram's horn that meant humility and strength.

An intriguing bird figure caught my eye. The bird's neck was turned, looking behind itself over its back. My mother would've adored this, especially since she called me magpie. I picked up the bird, half expecting it to smell of lemon. "What does this one mean?"

Philomel nodded as if in approval. "Return and get it," he said.

"I don't understand."

"Return to the past. Learn from the past. Never forget the ancestors who have already gone away from us."

I swallowed. *Oh.*

My stomach was so full.

Return and get it.

But I couldn't return, now could I? My mother was gone. I sniffed.

Philomel looked alarmed.

"I miss my mother," I squeaked out.

When he nodded, I remembered. *Oh that's right, he misses his mother too. He's an orphan after all.* It made me feel worse not better.

Tears ran down my face and my nose ran. I set the bird down and said, "I'll come back later. I do want to buy them."

Philomel grabbed my wrist as I stood. He pressed the bird into my palm. "Take this, Hah-nah. Keep it to remember your mother."

I shook my head, wishing desperately for a Kleenex. "No, I will pay you."

"This is my gift," he said.

"No, you made this. You worked hard on it."

"Please receive my gift."

I paused.

"You may give *me* a gift another time," he suggested.

I nodded, wiping my nose on my arm. "I will! I will!"

I already knew what it would be. I had a feeling Philomel would appreciate my cities.

The bird burned in my palm all the way back to my room. Thank God the house was empty, with everyone still at the party. I sat on the floor, leaned against my bed, and wept.

You'd feel so much better.

"Shut up!" I said.

I dug into my duffel bag for my purple notebook. In the back of it, I'd tucked a picture of my mother.

I looked at her sweet, open face. She crouched in our backyard, coffee cup in hand, looking at one of my cities. I'd called her name and she'd laughed to see the camera.

She wore the pink cashmere cardigan.

I pulled the cardigan out of my duffel and breathed in. Hints of lemon still clung to it. I rubbed its downy fuzz on my cheek.

50. Cashmere against your skin

Dr. Giulia Florio had asked me to write down "things that give you pleasure, you know, memories of simple, tactile sensations that soothe you" and had encouraged me to turn to those things when a binge was coming on.

Who are you kidding? Touching cashmere isn't going to make you feel as good as a binge!

I pushed my sweat-slick arms into the sweater sleeves. What else, what else?

63. Blowing soap bubbles
64. Blowing bubblegum bubbles
65. Those great vivid first seconds of a brand new piece of bubblegum

I tore through my duffel. No bubblegum, but there were packs of Chiclets, the third-world gum it seemed, just as Fanta seemed to be the third-world soda. I popped one of the flat white tabs into my mouth and relished the first crunch into its hard shell.

No good. Within seconds I'd sucked it flavorless. I went through a whole box, crunching, sucking the sweetness from the tab, spitting it out, trying another.

Nothing is going to make you feel better. You know it's true.

I skimmed through the list.

26. The way your skin smells when you've been in the sun

I pushed back the cashmere and pressed my nose to my

forearm, but only smelled the smoky goat stew and my own sweat.

71. Sand under your bare feet

No good. No sand here. Landlocked in Tafi Atome.

98. Catching a snowflake on your tongue
99. Laughing so hard you cry
100. Lambs

These are worthless! Just give in. Just do it.
No, no, no.
I jumped from page to page.

27. Pirates
33. Tandem bikes
57. Icing sugar cookies
77. Root beer floats
82. Popping bubble wrap

Bubble wrap! I had bubble wrap! The woodcarver had given me bubble wrap to wrap some of my beads. I popped each little sac until the plastic sheet was flat and flimsy in my hands.

Then I gave up.

I opened a bottle of water, chugged it empty, then followed the jungle path to the outhouse. I couldn't vomit here. It wouldn't drain. I listened to flies buzz in the troughs a moment, then went behind the stone building. I bent over and tapped the back of my throat.

I gagged but didn't vomit, which surprised me.

I leaned over again. The tap made me heave, but nothing came up from my stomach. I coughed and sputtered, then gasped to catch my breath.

"Hah-nah?"

Modesta's voice made me jerk. I hadn't heard her footsteps on the path.

"Oh, Hah-nah." Her voice shamed me with its kindness. She put a hand on my back. "Did the meat make you sick?"

"No! No. That's not it." I leaned against the outhouse wall. Monkeys chattered overhead.

I looked at Modesta's short, burgundy hair—the color, Izzy had told me, was from malnutrition. Dimple's words came back to me. If vegetarianism was harsh and indulgent here, what words could describe what *I'd* been about to do?

"I will make you a tea to settle your stomach," Modesta said.

I shook my head. "I was just…I was upset. I was missing my mother."

Stern stoic Modesta hugged me. The love delivered from her bony arms made me miserable. We stood there in the forest, insects and monkeys chirring all around us, outside a toilet, and held each other.

"Oh," Modesta said, something like surprise and delight combined in her voice. She pulled back a bit. "Oh," she said again. She ran her hands down my arms, rubbing the pink cardigan.

"Isn't that a wonderful feeling?" I asked, looking at her dark hands on the pale pink. "It's called cashmere."

"Cashmere," she whispered. From the look in her eyes, you'd think she was having a religious experience.

The sticky heat itched at me. "Would you like to wear it? It feels really good to have it on your skin."

She nodded and let me drape her in it. My mother had been a petite woman, but the cardigan hung on Modesta in folds, making her look like Dopey, the dwarf from *Snow White*, especially when she pulled up the hood and pressed the cashmere to both cheeks.

I laughed. "You just wear that for a while," I said.

We walked back to the house, monkeys tumbling across the path ahead of us. "I will make you tea," she said again.

"No, no," I said. "No, thank you. I don't think—I don't think that will make me feel better."

She stopped, the hood of the cardigan a little pointed peak on top of her head. "What will?"

I thought about that. I felt better already. Better because I felt the breeze on my skin again. Better because I'd beaten her, Bulimia. For once. This time. I *hadn't* purged and no longer *wanted* to.

Before I could answer, she grinned. "You wish to email the boy worth liking? The one who is beautiful inside?"

I couldn't help but laugh. But I shook my head.

There was one person I wanted to talk to more than Jasper at the moment. One person who I truly knew would understand this small victory better than any other person besides Aunt Izzy.

I went to the empty schoolhouse, sat in the rickety little chair, and typed in my dad's email address.

Chapter 21

It felt so good to tell my dad about my battle won. For the first time, I felt like we might be on the verge of understanding each other. I told him about the lost-wax bird, of missing Mom, of all the things I'd done to try to divert... and of the giving in.

As I typed, it struck me that I hadn't really conquered Bulimia myself; I'd been interrupted by Modesta...but I knew if I'd still really *wanted* to purge, I would have. Modesta gave me the perfect excuse: that the meat had upset my stomach. Poor fragile little American pansy? Who wouldn't have bought that story? I didn't know if Dad would get it, but I knew that, by the point Modesta left me, I hadn't *needed* to purge. That's what made it a real victory.

When an email arrived from Jasper, my heart fluttered just looking at his name. Why hadn't I recognized my attraction to Jasper immediately?

I thought about Jasper, picturing him at the piano at school. School. Oh, *that* was why: Because I didn't recognize *myself* at school. Because I'd let my true self get hijacked.

School. I looked around the little schoolroom, at the open-air windows, the rudimentary chairs and desks. I pictured the B-Squad here. That was funny...except I would hate to subject the good people of Tafi Atome to those girls. Brooke *here?* No mirrors, no flush toilets, heck, no toilet *paper* (unless you'd brought your own, as we had). Goats under your bed. No screens. Monkeys who stole things from you. (The day before, I'd had to scramble to take an unopened tampon back from a monkey who'd spied it in my bag. Tampons were treasure here! I'd wrestle a monkey to keep it if I had to.)

My period was back, for the first time in over a year.

What if a monkey stole Brooke's tampon? How long before she was reduced to tears?

I never had been. Wow. I thought back—all the craziness, that scary first night, the goat. I'd never cried. The only thing that had reduced me to tears was the memory of my mother.

I'd told Jasper everything about Tafi Atome and the wonderful people who lived here. I'd sent him pictures of everything too—my room, my aunt, "my" goat, the water pump, the school. I took pictures inside the school, showing him the computer I used, and the plastic Tupperware box that went over it when it was not in use.

He commented on that photo. *What's on the shelves behind the computer? It looks almost empty, but what are those books?*

I hadn't even paid attention. Three books stood on the shelf: a battered hardback of *Little Women*, a paperback of *Tom Sawyer*—the pages soft as flannel—and *Runaway Bunny*.

Modesta told me, "That is our library. Every person in Tafi Atome has read these books."

I'd brought some books with me to read on the plane. I'd already finished two. I gave them to her, saying she could read them first, but then I'd love for them to go to the library. She acted as if I'd given her a million-dollar grant.

I told Aunt Izzy and the crew, and they all dug through their own luggage to produce seven books, a *National Geographic*, and three *Newsweeks*. We'd brought the library from three titles to thirteen books and three periodicals.

It's a good thing I took a photo of the "complete collection" when I did, since the library shelves were scooped bare at the first whisper of the new books.

I relayed all this to Jasper in my next email, thanking him for being so observant because his one question had made a huge difference in this little village.

He emailed back: *Wow. I can't imagine a life without books. Trying to feels like having an arm amputated. You know what? I haven't been able to figure out my Make a Difference Project. I think this decides it. I'm going to do a book drive for your village library. Could you send an address?*

Wow. What a good idea.

Imagining a life without books feels like having an arm amputated.

I thought of my own ignorant wish to be disfigured.

Englebert said Modesta was like the mother rabbit in *Runaway Bunny.*

Modesta smiled and said she wanted to write a book like Jo in *Little Women* about her adventures as a doctor. That book had made her want to do something with her life to be proud of.

What did *I* want?

I'd wasted too many years of my life wanting to be skinny.

Dad's next email was great. "Congratulations, Hannah, on a successful battle with your demon. I'm so proud of you."

Chills shimmied down my back, even though I sat in the oven of a room, no breeze to speak of. When had my dad last said that to me? I'd felt like all I'd done was disappoint and embarrass him with my ugliness, my weight, my stealing, my inability to get myself together.

I'm so proud of you.

That was weight loss; reading those words, I felt one hundred pounds lighter. Like I might float away.

He wrote more: *I've won some battles too. Some just barely. Remember: you don't have to do it on your own. You can ask for help. That's not a sign of weakness, but a sign of strength.*

Turns out Dad was still in the vampire movie! *I won't always get second chances like this*, he wrote, *so I can't blow it.* Because of his court orders, there were lots of stipulations and limitations, but the producers had agreed to all of them—Dad could only film in L.A., he had to be available for random sobriety tests, and he had to be free when I got off school. *The court didn't demand that one. I did. Not that you need babysitting, but I want to be there for you. I'm sorry for not getting it right, for not understanding your bulimia. I knew you were in trouble and I didn't know how to help you. It was easier to just numb myself out, to feel nothing rather than to feel that pain of failing you. There's nowhere more important for me to be than with you.*

We'd be back together in the same house, but without Mom. That would be hard.

Back together, though, and able to tell the truth to each other. That would be new. My bulimia would be out there, not a secret stinking away under the rug. Now that the truth was out, I had nothing to hide behind. I'd have to be pretty damn brave.

Jasper emailed to tell me how things were going with his Make a Difference Project: *All I had to do was send some emails and make one announcement at school. I already have more books than I know what to do with! The real issue is going to be shipping them. I had no idea how expensive it would be to ship books (which are heavy...duh) to Africa. I had a day of thinking I couldn't do it. I told DeTello I'd made a mistake, but she gave me a ton of ideas for help. Do you think that woman has ever given up on anything?*

I thought about that. Nope. Nope, I couldn't picture her ever saying, "I can't do this."

She was the sort who "jumped in with both feet," as Aunt Izzy said.

Hey, wait a minute…Izzy and my mom used to say that of *me!*

What do you think you're going to do? Jasper asked me. *People's ideas say a lot about them, I think. Kelly's raising money for something called Project HOPE. They provide school tuition, uniforms, and books to kids from Sierra Leone who are now orphaned. Did you know $100 will pay tuition and expenses for one kid there for a whole year? Don't you wish our tuition was that cheap?*

I'd never thought about what our tuition cost. I thought about Kelly with her vintage dress and high-tops; what a cool idea she'd come up with.

Brooke is petitioning to install mini-lockers in the bathrooms so girls don't have to carry all their 'beauty products' around.

I laughed out loud, frightening away a monkey who'd crept into the window sill. Beauty products? Other than shampoo, soap, and some sunscreen, I had no beauty products here. I'd asked Modesta if she had a mirror the other day and she'd snorted as if I'd asked her if she had a big-screen TV.

Brittany is raising money to buy the school lounge chairs so we can tan comfortably during lunch. I've already heard Brittany say her mom is just going to buy the lounge chairs because she doesn't want to deal with a bake sale or something! The whole point is we're supposed to raise the money ourselves, by giving something of ourselves, right? DeTello doesn't want us to just write a check, but to learn to "be the change we want to see." Oh, Kevin is petitioning to start a school surf team. What do you think about that? There are some who "get it," like Kelly. Amy is raising money for the Chinese orphanage she was adopted from, some kids have organized teams for beach cleanup, Sam is starting a recycling program at school (can you believe we don't have one?), and Laurie is doing a way cool project: she's organizing an urban garden in some empty lots near the school to raise produce for local food pantries.

I felt a twinge at the way he wrote about Laurie's "way cool" project. I recognized it with surprise. Jealousy. I wanted Jasper to see *me* as way cool. I shook my head. What did I expect?

Did he tell me the Kevin project on purpose? To paint Kevin in a bad light? Ha, like any painting was needed! There was no light worse than what Kevin had already cast himself in. But did Jasper wonder if I still liked Kevin? Had Jasper ever heard any of those gross lies of Kevin's from the pool party?

I decided not to say anything about Kevin, one way or the other, even though I wanted to say, "Who gives a monkey's butt what Kevin does for his project or anything else?" That day in the art room still made a weight settle on my chest.

Instead I wrote, *So, when did you realize there was a world beyond your own? What was the moment Jasper Jones recognized he was part of a bigger world than his own experience? I know the exact moment when I realized it. I think I was six.*

I would've written him the story then and there, but I'd already been at the computer for an hour. I didn't want to be the self-absorbed American hog.

I thought about my story for Jasper as I helped Aunt Izzy and the crew that afternoon.

I thought about my story for Jasper as I helped Modesta prepare dinner for the children.

I caught myself at one point doodling Jasper's eye, drawing that lighter, golden slice.

We were winding down to only a few days left in Tafi Atome, so I got busy. I gathered all my beads, shells, and trinkets, some of Philomel's coal clay, and some beer and Fanta cans. A whole day went by as I worked on a wooden table behind the Children's House, sweat dripping into my eyes and beading on my top lip. Monkeys jeered at me from the trees above. Twice I was so engrossed that a monkey was able to swipe items off my table; one was just a beer can that he tossed back from a tree later, but the other was a pretty cool shell. Ah, well. I tried to stay vigilant and shoo them away after that.

I built a miniature African market on a 16x20 piece of cardboard Modesta managed to wheedle for me from the village's only café (nothing got thrown away here; everything was of value and could be used). This was the smallest project I'd ever done, but I knew I didn't have much time. I made four rows of market stalls from clay, then augmented some of their walls with colorful tin cut from the cans—orange, green, brown, and purple. Other stalls were augmented with sticks, and some with small pebbles. Inside each stall I arranged items for sale: a pyramid of yellow and green beads for lemons and limes, seashells, bottle caps filled with painted rice to be plates of red-red, tiny sacks (cut from an old T-shirt of mine) stuffed with dirt, tiny bundles of dried grass and twigs. I framed one door of a stall with chicken bones to represent a voodoo market. I chopped up a chicken feather to glue a pile of miniature feathers there, and used the feather stem to make a pile of bones. Some stalls sold heaps of my most colorful tiny beads, and some stacks of fabric (folded piles of every scrap I could find, many of them trimmed from hems of my own clothing). I salvaged everything usable from my duffel and trash. To finish it off, I put five of Philomel's brass people in the aisles. It was a rush job, but when I wiped my sweaty face and stood back, it looked pretty darn cool, if I did say so myself.

I rolled my shoulders, wincing at the sunburn on the back of my neck, then carried the board—the city on top of it like some insane cake—to where Philomel chopped firewood near the water pump.

His eyes widened when I presented it to him. He peered at it, moving himself all around to look down one aisle and then another. He examined it from every angle and I knew the craftsman in him admired it. "Hah-nah, you made a little world here. This is good. This is a good gift. I thank you."

I then bought every last one of his brass people and a handful of brass animals as well—the two cloth bags I carried away were heavy.

But I felt light.

The real Hannah had broken free.

Chapter 22

The next morning, at the end of my run, I came upon Aunt Izzy sitting on a log. I thought she was crying, with her head in her hands, but when she heard my footsteps she lifted her head and I saw she had just been deep in concentration.

"You okay?" I asked, panting before her.

She nodded. "Just thinking about what's next."

"In the documentary?"

She made a face then nodded again.

"I thought you were really happy about how it was going and the footage you got this time."

"I am," she said, scooting over so I could use the end of the log to stretch. "I feel good. Hopeful. But...every time we come back from shooting, there's this horrible, frantic period of editing, more writing, raising money. I believe in this project so much, but every time we get home I have this fear that I can't pull it off."

I'd never heard someone grown-up admit something like this before.

"So how do you keep going?"

A monkey swooped down to snatch my sunglasses, but I clamped my hands down on them in time. We laughed.

Aunt Izzy looked up. The morning sun shone pink through the leaves. The monkey screeched at us. I'm sure he was cussing me out in monkey language.

"If I sit outside," Aunt Izzy said, "somewhere green in nature, there's this inner voice I hear. That voice believes in the project. When I listen to her, I keep the faith."

I pulled my right foot up behind me in a quad stretch. "I hear that voice when I run."

Izzy smiled. "Good. Keep listening to her."

When had I first heard that voice? That voice had been around long before I ran.

I thought about that voice as I "showered" behind the outhouse. That was the voice I'd had in childhood—curious, hungry to know everything about the world. The voice of an explorer. A bold adventurer. The very first time I remember hearing her was the story I wanted to tell Jasper.

I dressed, then went to the school to email him. I was surprised—and more disappointed than I cared to admit—that there wasn't an email waiting from him. I wrote him anyway. *Still thinking of your answer? Here's mine: I was five or six when I first thought about a bigger world. Some construction was going on in our neighborhood and they were tearing up the street. I was fascinated watching the big machines rip up the blacktop. I was even more fascinated by what was underneath: these big rocks and small pebbles. Who knew that all this stuff had been under there all the time, with me walking and riding my bike and coloring with chalk on top of it? But then I saw one of the bulldozers drop an ordinary rock, very plain on the outside and about the size of a watermelon. When that rock hit the ground, it cracked open...and inside that plain old potato-looking rock were jewels. The inside of that rock was sparkling pink, with glittering black flecks all through it. That's when a little voice told me that if there were mysteries, surprises, and discoveries under my own street and inside every rock, then they could be every single place I looked.*

I'd held back for so long—not sharing my cities, not joining track, not using the school's climbing wall—that it felt like coming home to reveal my true self.

Jasper wasn't like anyone else I'd ever met. The way he said he couldn't tell the B-Squad apart? That's how I felt about all the other boys at my school now. Jasper was the only one who seemed unique, who seemed to be his own person.

What would happen when I returned to L.A.?

Half of me wanted to be there already, and the other half wanted that day to never come.

Philomel returned from the market and told me that tourists had loved my miniature version. He made big, animated gestures as he told me, "They all wanted to buy it, but I said no, it was a gift. They wanted to know if I would ever have more. They love it, Hah-nah."

I grinned. "Really?" I tried to make my mouth stop smiling but couldn't. "That's so cool."

"No, not so cool," he said, "because you are leaving and they will not get what they want. Money they would like to give me will remain in their pockets. So I have a favor to ask you. Can I make another world like you did? It is your project, you are the artist, but you will be gone, so these customers could not be your customers."

"Are you asking if you could use my idea, like as a model?"

He nodded, looking at the ground, hands stuffed in his faded pockets.

"Of course you can, Philomel! I'd be honored. On one condition, though: you have to promise that whenever you make one, you will think of me."

He waited as if he didn't think I was finished, then looked perplexed. "Think of you?"

"You have to remember me."

His eyes widened as if I'd suggested he had to picture me naked or something. "Are you crazy?" he asked. "I can never forget you. No one here can ever forget you."

I don't know why, but hearing those words felt like opening a gift. So much so that my eyes watered. Philomel looked wary and was probably thinking I was the biggest crybaby ever. Every time he talked to me I ended up crying over something.

I wasn't prepared, though, for how much I would cry the day we left Tafi Atome. How could only four weeks change my life so much?

The last night, I slept in Modesta's room. We pushed our mats close together so we could whisper without waking the smaller girls who shared this room. We lay on our backs in the sweltering heat and talked of our dreams for the future. Our wishes. Jasper and Philomel.

At some point late in the night, Modesta fell asleep. I looked at her in the moonlight that sliced through our open unscreened window. What a brave person. She'd lost so much. Life had been so unfair—why, for instance, did *she* have to cook and clean for the smaller ones? Who had decided that? But she never complained. She looked to the future with practical cheer.

I tried to picture Modesta being afraid to speak her mind to some of her peers here in this village. I had to put my arm over my mouth to keep from laughing aloud.

I didn't laugh, though, when I thought of her dream. How could she possibly afford to go to medical school? That was an entirely different thing than getting a craft apprenticeship in a nearby village. The worry that she might never realize her dream kept me awake.

We rose early, and as I packed, I gave her many things: a pink bra, a T-shirt from Sprinkles Cupcakes in L.A., a pair of earrings, a notebook, several pens, a box of Band-Aids.

She handed me a small cloth bag, about the size of a pound of flour. It rattled as I took it from her hands. Inside were beads galore, all colors, all shapes, some solid, some striped. "You make another little world, like you did for Philomel. You make it and remember us." The way she smiled, I knew Philomel had told her what I'd said.

"Are you crazy, Modesta?" I whispered. "I will never forget you."

She hugged me, and as she pulled away, my hands touched that soft, pink cashmere. I paused, hands stroking the cuffs.

She looked up at me, expectant. I knew it was the one item, of all my belongings, that she'd pick if I said she could keep one thing.

I looked down at my tanned hands on the pale pink. "This was my mother's," I whispered.

Modesta jumped under my hands. "Ah!" she said, beginning to wriggle out of the sweater. "Then you must take it with you."

I put my hands around her forearms to stop her. It took me a moment to speak. "I want…" I took a deep breath. "I want you to keep it." My eyes burned. "She would want you to keep it too." That was so true I *felt* it. I looked down at the sweater, rubbing the soft fabric, afraid if I looked at Modesta, I'd cry. "You are so alike. Two of the bravest women I know."

Modesta took my face in her hands and said, "She taught you well, then."

You know what? That felt more and more true these days: that I could be brave. Would I be able to hold on to believing that when I got back home?

"And that is why I want to give you this," Modesta said, pulling something from the pocket of her dress. She held one of Philomel's lost wax figures on the palm of her hand.

I hadn't seen this figure before. A five-sided star inside

a circle, the circle itself rimmed in curled rays or spokes. "*Sesa Wo Suban*," she told me, hanging the figure around my neck.

She saw the question in my eyes and shook her head as if to scold herself for forgetting I didn't speak that dialect. "I change or transform my life," she translated.

My breath stopped in my chest. I felt like she'd sensed what I was just thinking. I'd never even told Modesta about the B-Squad. How would I even begin to make it make sense to her?

"I love this," I told her. "I *need* this."

I carried my duffel bag toward the van on what felt like wooden legs.

There were tears, laughter, promises to return, to write, to stay in touch. I hugged everyone, all the children, beautiful Philomel, and finally Modesta.

"Sister," I whispered in her ear, holding her close. "*You have transformed my life.*"

She squeezed me tighter.

"You are so, so beautiful," I told her.

She wrinkled her nose, but then looked me in the eye and said, "Thank you. Do not forget that you are beautiful too."

The farther we drove from Tafi Atome on those rutted, red roads, and then on the highways, the more I vowed to hang on to the ways Ghana had changed me.

The film team checked into a hotel in Accra overnight, before our flight in the morning. I set my duffel on the twin bed and headed to the bathroom. Western toilets, I remembered, looking forward to that luxury.

I stopped in my tracks. There was also a *mirror*. I stared at myself.

The sun had tanned my skin light caramel, but the change in my appearance was more than that. I looked... rested. My eyes were clear, no purple shadows under them. My cheeks and neck were normal, no longer bulging with that sausage-stuffed puffiness. I looked clean and *real*. I looked like *myself* again.

I touched my fingers to the figure Modesta had given me.

I might be all right after all.

But my breath constricted at the thought of returning to all I'd escaped.

Just thinking of home, school, and Jasper made my pulse race, but not in the fun, fluttery way. What would happen now? How would it feel when we were face to face, two actual people in the actual world together, surrounded by the B-Squad?

I caught myself making an inventory of foods I could shovel in for a binge.

Did I have a prayer once I got back to L.A.? Was I going to fall right back into the same disgusting habits? Was I going to lose myself again?

I looked in the mirror at the brass figure hanging around my neck. I ran the pads of my fingers over the curlicue edges.

I nicked my finger on one of the rays.

Hmm, I thought, sucking the faintly metallic taste of blood from my finger. I hoped that wasn't a sign.

Chapter 23

I stood in baggage claim with my dad, heart racing. Although Modesta and I emailed each other at least twice a week, I hadn't actually *seen* her for two *years*. I felt like I might cry or dance…or both. I was already all aflutter about tonight and the nerve-wracking event ahead.

When I saw her coming around the corner with my Aunt Izzy, tears burned in my nose. She was so tall! We embraced, my hands registering the soft whisper of the new lilac cashmere sweater I'd sent her this year for Christmas.

Izzy and Dad embraced. They'd come a long way.

We all had.

Dad checked his watch. "We have time for lunch, but then we have to be back at the house."

"Are you crazy?" Izzy asked. "I can't eat! I'm too nervous. Aren't *you* nervous?" She poked Dad's shoulder.

Modesta cleared her throat. "*I* would very much like to eat something."

We all laughed. That settled it.

Back at the house, after picking my way through a Thai salad, the stylists arrived.

"I'm glad to be a documentary filmmaker on nights like these," Izzy joked to my dad. "No one expects me to look as glamorous as you."

The time flew by in a blur as we got manicures, our hair styled, and our faces made up. "We don't do this every day," I assured Modesta, "but the Academy Awards is a really big deal."

"This I know," Modesta said, sounding the slightest bit offended.

My father was nominated for Best Actor for *Blood Roses*, and Aunt Izzy's film *A Continent of Orphans* was nominated for Best Documentary. I was Dad's date. Modesta was Izzy's.

I wore a pale yellow silk gown that looked like a dress you'd go tango in—cut on the bias mid-shin, halter style—with some of my mother's diamond jewelry.

Modesta looked classic and stunning in a pale pink sheath.

Aunt Izzy wore a stylish, sexy plum gown.

And Dad—he looked like a movie star in his tux, you know? The old-fashioned, honest-to-goodness *stars*.

Jasper called to wish us luck just as our limo arrived. "We'll be watching," he promised. He was hosting an Oscar party at his house. "I can't wait to see what you're wearing."

"You'll probably see it again next year at prom," I told him, laughing.

I'd almost wrecked it with Jasper.

When I first got back to L.A., the house ambushed me. The bathroom, kitchen, and my bedroom taunted me with humiliating memories. Mom was everywhere—slipping in and out of rooms in the corner of my eye, in the shimmer of the sea glass door frame, in the scent of our lemon tree. Once Dad and I got over our excruciating silences and stuttering, peppy attempts at conversation, I'd emailed Jasper. My heart slammed against my ribs as I typed: *I don't think I can wait until Monday. I'd really love to see you, but without the B-Squad watching. Let me know and I'll give you directions.*

But when he wrote back, *Thanks for the invite, but that's okay. I'll see you Monday,* the words punched me in the stomach.

That's okay.

Did he not *want* to see me? Had I just made a fool of

myself? Had I misinterpreted everything? "Don't eat the monkey, don't eat the monkey," I told myself.

When I stepped into the front school hallway on noodle legs, the piano music ran over me like warm water. I clutched my books, working up the courage to walk into the piano lounge, but when I did, Jasper didn't even stand up. He said, "Welcome back," but he kept right on playing. The B-Squad showed up—Brooke greeted me with, "You're not so tubby, but did you forget how to dress?"—and Jasper took his sheet music and left.

He may as well have slapped me. Why wouldn't he talk to me?

I ignored Brooke and tried to follow him, but got stopped in the hall by Kevin Sampson.

"You're back," he said, glee in his voice. "I missed you." He licked his lips.

I jerked my arm, but he wouldn't let go of me.

Itch. Itch. Itch. I shuddered from the bugs on my skin. *Why did you think anything would change you, stupid, ugly girl? You know what you'll have to do to make these feelings go away.*

"Shut up and leave me alone!" I said too loudly. Heads turned.

"Suit yourself." Kevin held up his hands as if in surrender.

The tardy bell rang. I rushed to Jasper's homeroom in time for the door to close in my face.

That sensation occurred about a hundred times before lunch.

Everywhere I turned, Kevin leered at me.

The B-Squad taunted me.

Jasper ignored me.

What? Did you think he was your boyfriend? Fat chance. What made you think any normal, nice boy would want you? Jasper doesn't want to be seen talking to you, you idiot.

"Don't eat the monkey," I vowed. "Don't you *dare* eat that monkey."

In DeTello's class, I found Jasper sitting at a table talking to Laurie.

My cheeks heated up. I stood there, paralyzed. *Don't cry. Don't cry.* I wanted to fly back to Tafi Atome and never return. I knew how to be myself there. Being myself just backfired here.

May as well fire up the cook stove because that monkey was getting barbecued.

As my crappy luck would have it, DeTello made us form groups for something. Group work should be outlawed. It's nothing but torture.

I ignored the hissed, "Hannah! Back here!" from Brooke

and looked to Jasper. He walked to Laurie's table. Roland joined them. They needed a fourth. I took a tentative step... but Kelly got there first.

I got stuck in the B-Squad.

After class, I stalked into the cafeteria on autopilot. When Jasper caught up with me, I shot him a look.

"What's the matter?" he asked.

Like he really didn't know.

"Are you okay?" he asked.

Was he serious? I shredded lettuce. Shredding was fitting. Shredding felt satisfying.

"Oh," he said, "so now you won't even talk to me when it's just us?"

I gaped. "Talk to y—? I've been *trying* to talk to you all morning!"

His face shifted. "I really thought things would be different," he said.

Before I could say, "So did I," Pam stepped in and told us to speed things up.

I didn't say another word to Jasper. At the end of lunch, he threw his plastic apron in the trash and walked out.

I stood there a moment, facing a pile of tomato slices. *I should put these in a plastic container for tomorrow and get to class.*

But you're not going straight to class, are you? Don't you have a little stop to make first?

No. Don't do it. It's been over *a month*. Don't do it.

You'll feel better. You'll feel nothing.

Call Dad. Call Dad instead.

I picked up a tomato slice. I took a bite.

That's it. That's a start.

I ate the slice, then picked up another.

I ate a third slice, knowing I'd eat the whole pile. Then I took a giant jar of apple sauce off the shelf above me. First I used a serving spoon to shovel it out of the jar, but then I lifted the jar to my mouth and drank it. While I chugged, I looked around. There were hamburger buns. And a whole tray of cookies. There was cheese and—

"Hannah!"

I dropped the apple juice jar and it broke at my feet with a muffled, wet *whump*.

"Why do you do this?" Jasper stepped toward me. "Please," he begged. "Don't."

When his hands touched the bare skin of my arm, I bolted. I slid in the applesauce and almost fell, but regained my footing and fled for the restroom.

"Hannah!" he yelled after me. "I know where you're going!"

So what? Unless he was going to come in and physically stop me, I didn't care. I shut myself in a stall and leaned over.

After I threw up, I stood up, panting. I didn't feel a rush.

I didn't feel any tingles.

But I didn't feel *nothing*. I *still* felt anger and sorrow and betrayal.

I tried again, but not very much came up.

I tried again but couldn't breathe. Everything stuck for a minute. A minute? I don't know.

A *long time*.

Black spots burned in my eyes. Panic welled in my choked-close throat.

What should I do? Should I go out to the hall? Find someone to do the Heimlich? Call 9-1-1?

You need to breathe.

I could do the Heimlich on myself! I'd done it before.

For real. You need to breathe.

I fumbled with the lock on the stall door, but the black dots burned wider. I could only see on the edges of the circles.

You're going to die here. You're going to die in a toilet!

I gave up on the door, locked both fists together and slammed them into my own belly.

Nothing.

I did it again.

And again.

My throat exploded.

That's what it felt like. I projectile vomited across the stall, splattering myself.

You are filthy, vile, sickening.

I sucked in a honking breath, then swallowed wrong, the acid burning in my windpipe.

Something tickled my chin, dripping.

I wiped my chin, but it dripped again.

Oh God. I tried to look through the dots, at the edges. Red. Dark, burgundy red.

My nose was bleeding.

I groped for the toilet paper dispenser with slick hands.

The spattering sound on the tile floor made my heart race. My nose was really *gushing*.

"Hannah?" DeTello's voice. Concerned. Out of breath. *Underwater?* "Are you in here?"

"Yeah." I brought a giant wad of toilet tissue to my nose. It took a long time. The film had changed to slow motion.

The stall door rattled. "Open up. Are you all right?" DeTello's voice seemed far away.

I wanted to say *I'm fine*, but my mouth wouldn't work. I moved my head sideways to try to find the lock on the edges of the dots, but the edges were wavery and sparkly.

From deep down in a well, I heard DeTello say, "Hannah? Please, sweetie. Talk to me."

I *tried*. I tried to move my lips, but the sparkles got brighter and then I—

Getting to the nurse's office was a blur. Blurred by relief. I wasn't dead. I wasn't blind.

DeTello and the nurse cleaned me up. They dressed me in a stranger's sweatpants and a turtleneck from the lost and found. They made me drink Gatorade and eat two cookies.

I woke up forty minutes later on the nurse's cot, with my dad leaning over me, kissing my forehead. "Hannah Banana," he whispered. "Rough day?"

I nodded, a tear burning down my cheek. My throat felt shredded.

The nurse slipped out and closed the door, giving us some privacy.

"I wish I'd called you," I said. "I even thought about it, but…but I think I waited too long. To, you know, ask for help. It was too late."

He smoothed my hair. "I've been there. You'll do better next time. You'll be stronger."

Next time? Oh God, I didn't want there to *be* a next time.

I thought about my horrible day. Okay…there *might* be a next time. But the binge that day had been the first in a *long* time. Maybe the next one—*if* it happened at all—would be a longer time still. I'd learn each time, get stronger, get new strategies.

"What made the day so hard?" Dad asked. "Do you know what triggered the binge?"

Once I started, with the B-squad and Kevin and Jasper, I couldn't stop. Talk about a purge! I talked on and on, filling him in on the start at the new school and everything in between.

A few times Dad bristled and his eyes blazed, but he never interrupted me. When I finally came to a halt, and said, "I really liked Jasper. I thought he liked me too. I thought that he was different, but maybe he's as big a jerk as Kevin. Just in a different way."

Dad exhaled and said, "This Kevin you talk about, do I know him? Kevin who?"

"Yeah, you know him," I said, barely hearing my own voice. "You work with him."

"Kevin *Sampson?!* I'll kill him. Why didn't you tell me this?"

It was too hard to explain. Would it hurt Dad too much to know that I honestly thought he'd believe Kevin, not me?

I sighed. "I wasn't really thinking very rationally you know."

His shoulders slumped. "I do know," he said. "I know too well."

"You're not really going to kill him are you?"

Dad narrowed his eyes. "No. I won't kill him. But *only* because—"

I waited. When he didn't finish, I said, "What?"

"Only because I don't want to go back to jail," he admitted.

I threw my head back on the ugly green cot and laughed. It felt so, so good, even on my trashed throat.

Africa had been a distraction, not a cure. It was silly of me to think the struggle was over.

But I *wanted* it to be.

That was a new twist on this old, boring story.

Dad smiled and stroked my hair. "We're going to be all right, aren't we?"

I nodded. "I think we really are."

★✫★

Although we arrived at the Academy Awards in the same limo and would be seated together, Dad and I had to part from Izzy and Modesta for the red carpet gauntlet. We answered inane questions about our clothes and about Mom. "How does it feel to be here without her?"

What kind of moronic question is that? I wanted to scream. *How do you* think *it feels?*

"She's here in spirit," Dad would say each time.

I'd been coached for all this, just as Dad had prepared to be asked about the competition (he was up against his best friend, Sean, which the reporters loved).

When we finally got inside, we found our seats with Izzy and Modesta, the rest of the documentary team in the row behind us.

I was so proud of my friend sitting beside me. Although I found lots of the awards ceremony pretty boring, she seemed enthralled. We probably had four hours ahead of us to go, but I already wished I was at Jasper's house, in jeans instead of all dolled up.

Oh, that's right. Jasper. I told you how we almost blew it, but I didn't tell you how we fixed it. After that horrible first day back at school, after I'd relapsed, then passed out in the bathroom, Jasper showed up at my house.

I'd been out in the backyard. Dad was inside with Sean and Laila. I could've helped with dinner, but I felt fidgety. I dug around in the garage and unearthed a board about the size of a cookie sheet. I gathered my African supplies, found a bucket and mixed up the clay. I sat in the backyard—under the lemon tree—in dirt that was brown, not red, with no monkeys waiting to rob me. Instead of palm oil and cook fires, the air smelled of eucalyptus. I began to build another African market scene.

I got lost in it. So lost, the time slipped by again.

So lost, I didn't hear the back gate open.

So lost, I jumped big time when Jasper said, "Hey, Hannah," from right behind me.

"Whoa," he said. "I didn't mean to scare you. Your dad told me to put my bike back here."

I scrambled to my feet after crouching too long, so dizziness slammed me for the second time that day. I put out my hands, and Jasper caught me in a sort of rescue hug. "Are you okay?"

"Um, yeah," I said, blinking hard to bring the backyard back into sight.

The yard righted itself.

"I came to see if you were all right," Jasper said.

We stood, holding each other's hands as if we were about to dance.

I pulled away, confused. I found my voice, but it was thin and shaky. "I don't get it. If you care enough to come over and see if I'm okay, why wouldn't you talk to me this morning?"

He shoved his hands in his pockets. "You really hurt my feelings, Hannah," he said.

"*I* hurt *your* feelings?" I asked. "How?"

"Oh, come on. You said you only wanted to see me when the B-Squad wasn't around. How do you think that made me feel?"

The yard slanted. "*What?* When did I say that?"

"In your email on Saturday."

I thought back. I hadn't said that, had I? I tried to remember my wording. I closed my eyes. When I opened them, the yard slanted back to how it was supposed to be. This was fixable.

"Jasper, that's not what I meant at all. At *all*. I can see how you might've thought that, based on what I said. I typed it so fast, and I was kind of nervous. But, really, I just didn't want to *wait* until Monday. I wanted to see you as soon as I could."

He stood there, absorbing this. He took his time, just like he did in class. He tossed his hair out of his eyes. "Why were you nervous?"

Truth just kept spilling out of my mouth. "I was nervous because I really like you, Jasper, and I didn't want to make an idiot of myself if you didn't like me back."

"How could you think I didn't like you, based on our emails?"

"That's what I *thought*, but then this morning, I was so…oh my God, I was…*crushed*."

"I'm sorry," he said.

"I am too. But how could you think I didn't want to be seen with you based on *my* emails?"

He unfurled his grin. "I was nervous."

"Why were you nervous?"

He tossed his hair out of his eyes. "Because I really like you Hannah. I was scared to believe you liked me back."

I thought I might levitate.

He hugged me. For real this time.

The top of my head fit just under his chin. I closed my eyes. He smelled so good.

"Wow," he said when he ended the embrace. He looked down at the miniature market I'd been making.

We pulled apart, but he kept hold of one of my hands. My cheeks blazed. I wondered if Dad, Sean, and Laila were watching.

"This is amazing," Jasper said, real admiration in his voice.

He sat down cross-legged in the dry grass to look closer, his nose inches from the clay, beads, and aluminum. "You are so talented."

I laughed.

"And you look so…beautiful."

I stubbed my toe in the dirt. "Well, you know, a little visit to the third world can help you lose weight."

He looked baffled. "I'm not talking about weight. I'm talking about your face. Your...glow."

I didn't know what to do with my hands. He looked at me as intently as he had the market.

"It's the first thing I noticed this morning," he said. "You look...transformed."

I touched the brass figure on my breast bone. "I *am* transformed."

What I loved about Jasper is that he didn't take it as a joke. He nodded.

I sat down on the grass beside him. "I feel like the real me is back. The authentic me. I'm...happy. I haven't been happy for a long time." I couldn't think of a single other person my own age that I could share this with.

"Authenticity and happiness are the best beauty products out there."

He touched my cheek. I felt dizzy all over again. I put my hand over his and then held it. "Your emails meant so much to me," I said. "I was having a really hard time."

"I think that's probably an understatement."

That golden triangle hypnotized me.

"I don't just mean my mom"—God, I couldn't even say

it. Would that ever get easier?—"or my dad getting arrested. I was having a hard time before that. Those things"—things seemed the wrong word. Could you call your mother dying a "thing"?—"just made it worse, but like I told you, I have some issues."

Don't tell him! What are you doing?

"I could kinda tell, Hannah." His forehead scrunched up. "What happened today?"

I wanted to shrink and hide inside my miniature market. "I owe you an explanation of..."

He shook his head. "You don't owe me anything, Hannah."

"I want to be honest. You're always so real and honest."

"Well, okay," he said. "But don't tell me if you're not ready. It doesn't have to be today."

Don't tell him! He just gave you permission not to tell him!

I kept hold of his hand. I looked down at his hand and held it in both of mine, tracing those graceful fingers with my own. Then, I stepped off the cliff. "I have Bulimia."

Falling,

falling,

flailing in horrible free fall. I'd shatter on the rocks below, everything disgusting and revolting splattering out of me. This sweet, nice boy would find an excuse to leave.

I looked up at Jasper's face...and the free fall stopped. His face was still open and kind.

Not disgusted.

Not revolted.

Maybe a little sad. That's all.

I exhaled.

He squeezed my hand. "How'd that feel?"

"Terrifying," I admitted. I looked only at his hand when I asked, "You don't think it's gross?"

"Well...yeah, bulimia is pretty gross."

I stiffened.

"But *you* aren't gross, Hannah. There's a big difference."

He was right. Bulimia *was* gross. I marveled again that I'd missed how amazing he was when I'd first met him.

He took my hand and turned it palm down to rub that blister mark he'd noticed all that time ago. It was fainter, lots fainter, but still there. It had taken a while to build it up, so no doubt it would take a while to fade away.

I went inside and got Jasper his gift. I gave him the strip of kente cloth and told him all about the chief who'd taught me to bargain. "I thought maybe you could put that on your piano."

He ran his fingers over the fabric. "Someday, when I have my own piano, I certainly will."

"You don't have a piano?"

He shook his head. "That's why I practice at school all the time. Pam lets me in really early, before the school doors are unlocked. Dexter's let me in on weekends too."

"The more I learn about you, the more amazing you become."

He leaned forward, his face toward mine. Was he going to *kiss me?*

Panic made me duck my face, and I instantly regretted it. *Why? Why? You big chicken!*

He stood. "Now it's time for *your* gift." He went to his backpack on the ground near his bike and pulled out a long, flat box. As he walked back to me, I saw it was a See's Candy box. Now, See's Candy is very, very good, but…My smile tightened. You could give your teacher candy. You could give your grandmother candy. You could give *anyone* candy!

When he handed the box to me, it felt unusually heavy with my disappointment. "Thanks, Jasper." I forced my voice cheerful and perky.

He sat down beside me again. "Aren't you going to open it?"

"Oh! Would you like some?"

I didn't understand why he laughed until I opened the box.

Inside the box, in each of the little holes where a chocolate would go was a…rock.

"Take one," he urged.

I looked at his face, wary—was he mocking me?—but his expression was kind, eager.

I picked up one rock, but it was in two pieces. I held the top half and saw that inside this plain, gray rock were purple glittery sparkles. "Oh," I breathed.

The story. The story I'd told him, about realizing a bigger world existed. He'd remembered!

Jasper handed me the bottom half of the rock he'd picked up off the ground. In the space where the rock had been was a folded piece of paper, the size of a fortune from a cookie. I unfolded it and read the words, *You are a survivor.*

"You are the coolest guy alive," I whispered.

Each of the rocks held a startling surprise inside, and each had a paper underneath. *You are an incredible artist, You see the world in a unique way, I can tell you apart, You're authentic, Your hair is the exact color of honey, You're smart, You're funny, You can cut onions without crying, There is nothing fake about you,* and *You are brave.*

My very, very favorite one was the last one I unfolded. *You are beautiful inside and out.*

I swallowed. The lemon tree's aroma suddenly seemed overwhelming.

He tossed his hair out of his eyes. "You thought it was just a lame box of candy, didn't you?"

I laughed and nodded.

He leaned in again.

This time I didn't duck.

He tasted minty and warm. My legs dissolved even though I already sat down.

I would've kissed Jasper all day.

I would've kissed Jasper forever.

But my dad came out on the deck and yelled in an odd, high-pitched voice that didn't sound like him at all, "Hey, you guys! You want some dinner?"

129. Kissing

130. Perfect, unique, special personal gifts

131. A good run when you feel like you're floating

132. Being in love

133. Kissing

I thought about my first kiss, and all the kisses with Jasper since, as the awards ceremony crawled on.

At long last, the documentary category rolled around.

I had to remember that they occasionally panned the audience, and they would certainly show my dad and I while Aunt Izzy was up—everyone milked our connection for all it was worth.

I smiled, but I felt sick. It took forever for the actress in pink sequins to open the envelope.

Aunt Izzy won. She held Modesta's hand and led her up the stairs to the stage.

Izzy gave a witty, *quick* speech as she always did. Images from my time in Ghana flooded my brain. I swear I could even smell palm oil.

Izzy guided Modesta to the microphone where my friend spoke with poise as if she'd been doing this all her life. She thanked the glamorous crowd for caring about so many children without parents, for the attention and resources that would help these orphans be able to "lead our world into a better place."

I sat there inspired to make up for the time I'd wasted.

Because of Modesta, I'd finally come up with a Make a Difference Project.

Jasper had shown my cities to his parents. They'd shown my cities to his Aunt Sena who had a gallery in Silver Lake. His Aunt Sena showed my cities to some clients who wanted to buy them. Buy them for ridiculous prices.

When that first one sold, I told Dad my idea. "I want to help pay for Modesta's college."

His face was unreadable. I told him all about the Make a Difference Project, how this would be *perfect*, since if Modesta became a doctor, she'd end up helping a bunch *more* people. "It would get the most mileage, you know? The ripple effect would be huge."

Dad still didn't speak. I jabbered on, over explaining, because I didn't know what to make of his silence. "So, I could put all the money I make from selling the cities into an account for Modesta. I don't know how all that would work yet, how to get money to her and all, but we could figure that out, right? I probably couldn't pay for it all, but I could help. It would be nice if maybe for once she didn't have to work so hard, you know?"

I ran out of words. Dad stared at me. Was he even listening to me? Did he think it was stupid?

"Dad?" I whispered.

"Hannah," he choked out. "That's beautiful. That's so beautiful. I wish your mother were here to see this. She'd be so, so proud of you. You know what she'd say, don't you?"

I nodded. Now *I* was the one unable to speak. I *did* know what she'd say. But what I'd never known before, though, was that pretty was also something you could *feel*.

But Dad had more news for me that day. My mom left a trust for me. A pretty big trust. Dad and I thought maybe we could help more than just Modesta. We could start a scholarship in Mom's name for other girls too.

Modesta accepted our intervention on her behalf with a calm grace, but she had conditions of her own: she'd keep supplying me with Philomel's figures for my cities, as well as beads and other trinkets from Ghana. I'd received a monthly package from her for the last two years.

As it turned out, Modesta might not need as much help from us as I'd originally worried. Her high academic scores had already earned her the promise of a scholarship in Accra.

Speaking of...my high school track coach had hinted I could probably run for a college team if I wanted. We'd see. I wasn't sure if I wanted to keep running competitively, although I knew I'd run—for myself—until my legs couldn't do it anymore.

Bebe'd joined the track team too. We weren't, by any stretch of the imagination, real *friends*, but she was the first leg of the mile relay, and I was the last. She'd set a blistering pace, and I'd close any gaps the middle two legs allowed. Together we were unstoppable. She'd defected from the B-Squad a month or so after I did. That surprised me. I'd expected Brittany to leave, but she stuck by Brooke even now.

Leaving had been so much easier than I ever dreamed. Once I broke away, Brooke just ignored me. What had I really expected to happen? What had kept me afraid for so, so long?

Once Aunt Izzy collected her Oscar, the ceremony seemed to be moving at fast forward.

Best Supporting Actor came up.

Dad leaned over to whisper into my hair, "Remember, be polite. They might film our reaction if Kevin wins."

Oh, yeah. Did I forget to mention that? Kevin was nominated too. I guess I was just focusing on the *good* parts.

Kevin hadn't even *looked* at me at school for the rest of eighth grade. The first time I saw him after that nurse's office talk with Dad, Kevin froze in his tracks. I swear the expression that crossed his face was *fear*. He practically fled from me. I begged my dad to tell me what he'd said to Kevin, but he always stuck to his story: "I just told him to leave you alone."

"But *how* did you say it? What did you *do?*"

He'd sigh and laugh, then step close to my face and half-whisper like Clint Eastwood, "Leave my daughter the hell alone."

And Kevin had *done* it.

Then, this past summer before we were sophomores, Kevin had caused a drunk driving accident of his own. His scandal splashed all over the tabloids and entertainment shows. His parents hustled him into rehab.

One day last fall, Dad had come into my room and said, "I know you're no fan of Kevin. And I'm not either. But I think I might be able to help him. I'd like to go talk to him in rehab, if that's okay with you."

I couldn't believe Dad was asking my permission, but I loved him for it.

I kind of understood why Dad had wanted to help Kevin too.

I'd felt the same way about Brooke.

Brooke had changed freshman year, and not for the better. I'd been forced to be her lab partner once and had seen the faint scars on her forearms as she handled the microscope. Whatever. I hadn't lost too much sleep over it, but months later I came across her in the bathroom during a class period (I was in there, honest to God, to simply pee). She stood at the sink, shirt hiked up exposing her midriff, a paper towel pressed to her ribs. The terror on her face when she wheeled to see who it was broke my heart. "What are you staring at?" she'd asked.

I could've said, "I'm staring at the bloody paper towel you're holding."

I could've said, "I'm staring at the fact that you obviously hurt yourself."

I could've said, "I'm staring at the fact that you have a serious problem."

But I didn't.

I just shut myself in a stall to pee.

When I came out, the red-splotched paper towels on top of the trash were the only evidence she'd been there.

Weeks later, I went to the counselor to explain what I knew. It was then I understood why Dad had gone to see Kevin.

Once you've been there yourself, once you've been so lost, miserable, and fumbling, and you've managed to crawl your way out, you can't help but want to help others who are as buried as you once were. No matter how hideous she'd been to me, I knew what she was going through was *more* hideous. She'd just chosen a different way of hurting herself than I had.

At the Oscars, they showed a clip of Kevin from *Blood Roses* and I fell for it *again*, just like I had when I'd seen the full film. When I'd attended the premiere with Dad, I'd tried to resist liking Kevin's performance at all, bracing myself to criticize it later. But the creep was very talented. I believed every word he said on screen. And those eyes—those eyes that had filled my brain with white noise—well, their affect was amplified on the big screen. It wasn't fair. Why should someone so scummy get so much talent?

I caught myself clapping at the end of the clip in spite of myself.

Guess who won?

I rose to my feet along with Dad, smiling and clapping, even though I seethed inside. I'd wanted *anyone else* in that category to win besides Kevin.

As Kevin went to the podium, Modesta leaned toward me and said, "He is beautiful."

I made a face and whispered, "Only on the outside."

Modesta raised her magnificent eyebrows. I saw her remembering our conversation at the village pump. She tipped her head toward Kevin asking, *Him?*

I nodded.

Dad tapped my knee. *Be polite.*

Kevin at the podium wasn't at all like the Kevin in the swimming pool…but, then again, he was an *actor* and very skilled at pretending to be someone else. As he thanked everyone who had helped him, he was humble and even sheepish.

"But there's one person I need to thank above all others," Kevin said, drawing to a close. His voice grew husky. "I don't think I'd be alive today if it weren't for Caleb Carlisle."

I felt as if the breath had been punched out of my stomach.

Dad squeezed my hand. *The cameras are on us*, he was reminding me.

"Caleb is a survivor," Kevin said. "An amazing man. He stepped up to the plate when I was in trouble and even though he didn't have any reason to—and believe me, he *really* didn't have any reason to"—this he delivered with a self-deprecating laugh—"he *helped* me. He's a great actor and an even greater man and I will always, *always* be grateful to him. Thank you."

The place went wild. Standing ovation. I knew that the ovation was for my father, not just Kevin.

When we went to commercial break, Modesta said, "That was beautiful," of Kevin.

"Yes," I had to agree, "it was."

★★★

Finally, finally, as we grew terrifyingly close to the fourth hour of the ceremony, the Best Actor category was called. Third to last, with only Best Director and Best Film to go. I thought I'd felt sick over the documentary, but it was nothing compared to the I'm-so-nervous-I-can't-breathe-or-swallow sensation that gripped me now.

They showed the clips. Oh, man, every single actor was so, so good. But please, oh, *please* let my dad get this!

He didn't.

It's so weird how everything leading up to a certain moment can be so intense, so crucial, so life-or-death—this feeling of he *has* to win. It's the only thing that can happen!

Then it doesn't.

And you know what?

Everything is okay.

When they announced that Sean had won this year's award for Best Actor, I looked at my dad and he was genuinely happy for his best friend.

But more importantly, I looked at my dad and saw he was genuinely happy *in general*.

So was I.

Even better was the fact that, as we looked at each other, I knew we were thinking the same thing. We were happy. We'd survived.

We didn't need a little bald gold man to tell us that.

★☆★

You know what else I realized later, after we finally left the parties where Dad had to put in an appearance, and met up with Izzy and Modesta back at Jasper's house? I didn't need my list anymore either.

Oh, don't get me wrong. I'm not throwing it away. It's

a wonderful reminder of all I have to be grateful for. But as I stood there, overflowing with happiness, accepting a kiss from my smart, funny boyfriend, I knew there were *too many* reasons to write down.

> Having a tribe of good family and friends
>
> Helping someone
>
> Accepting help yourself
>
> Forgiving someone
>
> Forgiving yourself

Someone snapped a picture of me with Jasper. *Feeling beautiful.*

So, so many reasons right here in this room.

> Buttered popcorn
>
> Theme parties
>
> Jasper's big fat cat Jazz
>
> The Parmesan-artichoke dip Jasper's mom makes
>
> Putting on a pair of cozy jeans after being dressed up too long
>
> Sitting with a bunch of friends snuggled on a couch with
> your legs all entwined

But the most important one? *Knowing who you are.*

"Hey, we should make a toast!" I called. I raised my Sprite. "In Modesta's beautiful words, here's to 'leading our world into a better place.'"

Making a difference.

Have I put *Kissing* on my list?
Let's not forget *kissing*.

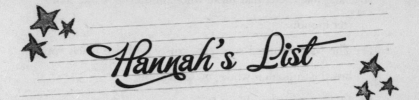

Hannah's List

1. Swimming with dolphins
2. Outrunning a forest fire
3. A hot air balloon ride
4. Seeing a shark fin while surfing but making it back to the shore intact
5. Hiking by moonlight
6. Making lists
7. Jumping on a trampoline in the rain
8. Ghost stories
9. Painting your toenails
10. Winning a race
11. Dark chocolate melting in your mouth
12. Pad Thai so spicy hot it makes your nose run
13. The way frosted grass crunches under your feet
14. Big wool sweaters
15. Exploring attics and basements

16. Fang-like icicles that make whole houses look like monster mouths

17. The way a knitted scarf gets crusty with ice when you breathe through it while you're sledding

18. Making snow angels

19. The Styrofoam squeak your shoes make on really cold snow

20. The smell of Band-Aids

21. Cat purr vibrating through your skin

22. Hiking with Dad up on Arroyo Seco and seeing a mountain lion at dusk

23. Vampires

24. Playing with the rubbery residue after you let glue dry on your fingers

25. Running my hands through a barrel of beads

26. The way your skin smells when you've been in the sun

27. Pirates

28. Aunt Izzy's purple house

29. An ice cream cone on a really hot day

30. Ice cold milk and Oreo cookies

31. Rainbows

32. Naps just because you have time to take them

33. Tandem bikes

34. Postcards from friends in cool places

35. Beach glass

36. Orange bougainvillea

37. Really great thrift stores

38. Chocolate-dipped strawberries

39. Rock climbing

40. The way ducks sound like they're chuckling

41. The scent of vanilla

42. Revenge movies

43. The word "peevish" (I just like it)

44. Manatees

45. The way patriotic marches played by whole orchestras make me feel like I'm going to cry

46. Flannel sheets

47. Wearing pajamas to school

48. The word "serendipity"

49. Finding surprise stuff inside boxes at yard sales

50. Cashmere against your skin

51. Sleeping in on rainy mornings

52. Real whipping cream

53. Silly Putty

54. Slinkies

55. Hammocks

56. Running hurdles when you hit your stride just right

57. Icing sugar cookies

58. Lemon meringue pie

59. Gnawing on buttery crab legs, feeling like a real carnivore

60. Catching a fish

61. Old-fashioned keys (and wondering what they open)

62. Sun through stained glass windows

63. Blowing soap bubbles

64. Blowing bubblegum bubbles

65. Those great vivid first seconds of a brand new piece of bubblegum

66. Finally seeing a trailer for a movie you've been waiting for

67. That screeching sound of packing tape

68. Dogs wearing sweaters

69. Finger painting (especially when you know you're "too old" to be doing it)

70. The smell of Play-Doh

71. Sand under your bare feet

72. Seeing a shooting star

73. Riding the front car of a roller coaster

74. Raw cookie dough

75. Glitter

76. Watching documentaries

77. Root beer floats

78. The smell of crayons

79. Blowing out birthday candles

80. Extra stuff after the credits at the movies

81. Those cool old-fashioned diaries with locks and keys

82. Popping bubble wrap

83. Autumn leaves changing color

84. Haunted houses

85. Making jack-o'-lanterns

86. Trick-or-treating

87. Wearing a costume

88. The scuttle sound autumn leaves make on the sidewalk

89. Getting yourself all freaked out after a scary movie

90. Warm, fluffy towels straight out of the dryer

91. The skin on top of pudding

92. That smell when the first drops of rain hit concrete

93. Dancing like an idiot when no one is watching

94. Cinnamon and sugar on butter-soggy toast

95. Rubbing velvet the wrong way

96. Remembering dreams

97. Playing hooky with Mom

98. Catching a snowflake on your tongue

99. Laughing so hard you cry

100. Lambs

101. The sound of water lapping on the shore

102. The way Mom gave me butterfly kisses with her eyelashes when I was little

103. That lemon meringue lotion she used, so she always smelled like dessert

104. The way she called me beautiful

105. The way she'd actually listen

106. Mom's smile when I walked into the room

107. The way she called me Hannah Banana

108. The look on her face the times I watched her studying my cities when she didn't know I was looking

109. Our beach glass door frame in moonlight

110. Mom's dorky birthday poems

111. The way Mom sang off-key to the car radio

112. The way Mom always smiled and never rushed her fans when they approached her

113. Dreams where my mom is still alive and healthy

114. BLUE ICING!

115. Being safe

116. Having a home

117. Never having been physically harmed by anyone

118. Having my entire body intact

119. The sounds of the rain forest at night

120. Fresh, hot (from the sun) pineapple out of the shell

121. Friends you can trust

122. Children singing in another language

123. Doing something you haven't done in a really long time that you've really missed

124. Having more than you need

125. Seeing an elephant (not in a zoo)

126. Drum music

127. Weaver birds

128. That mouthwatering, stomach-growling aroma of grilling meat

129. Kissing

130. Perfect, unique, special personal gifts

131. A good run when you feel like you're floating

132. Being in love

133. Kissing

134. Finding a live starfish and tossing it back in the water before it's too late

135. Watching Dad bake fresh bread

136. The aroma of rosemary

137. Finding money you forgot about in your coat pocket

138. Sprinkles Cupcakes in Beverly Hills

139. Sun-dried laundry

140. The cool side of the pillow

141. Snapdragons

142. Girl Scout cookies

143. Spending hours in a book store

144. Receiving handwritten, personal mail

145. Receiving handwritten, personal mail from a foreign country

146. Sunday morning waffles

147. Fun jitters on race days

148. Hiking in the rain

149. Sleeping under the stars

150. Picnics

151. Polka dots

152. The smell of leather

153. Working your butt off for a test, then acing it

154. Cute videos of kittens when you're having a stressful day

155. Fireworks

156. When your favorite song comes on in the car

157. White water rafting

158. Building sand castles

159. Indian food

160. Learning to make Indian food yourself

161. Learning a foreign language

162. The sound of anyone speaking Italian

163. Making homemade ice cream

164. Dr. Seuss

165. Cool museums

166. Splashing in puddles

167. Field trips from school!

168. Really good hair days

169. Beating your personal best in track

170. Sitting in a hot tub after running

171. Full body massages

172. Pumpkin pie

173. Roasting marshmallows over a campfire

174. Old photo albums

175. Puppies

176. The aroma of coffee

177. Hot cocoa with little marshmallows

178. Watching old black-and-white movies

179. Cotton candy

180. Ferris wheels

181. Henna tattoos

182. Finding a four-leaf clover

183. Love letters

184. Feeling strong

185. Trapeze artists

186. Homemade Valentines

187. Eating with chopsticks

188. Sushi

189. Wasabi

190. Holding Sean and Laila's newborn baby

191. The sound of a baby laughing

192. The sound of my father laughing

193. Watching the Olympics

194. The thick, sweet syrup at the bottom of a Sno-Cone

195. Eating peanuts at a baseball game

196. Jasper's music

197. Good movie versions of your favorite books

198. When dewdrops hang on spider webs and look like diamonds

199. New Year's resolutions

200. A kiss at midnight on New Year's Eve

201. Fog

202. People-watching in airports

203. People-watching at zoos

204. That sweet anticipation waiting to see someone you love in an airport

Having a tribe of good family and friends

Helping someone

Accepting help yourself

Forgiving someone

Forgiving yourself

Feeling beautiful

Buttered popcorn

Theme parties

Jasper's big fat cat Jazz

The Parmesan-artichoke dip Jasper's mom makes

Putting on a pair of cozy jeans after being dressed up too long

Sitting with a bunch of friends snuggled on a couch with
your legs all entwined

Making a difference

Kissing

Acknowledgments

My Reasons to Be Grateful (in no particular order):

1. My wonderful parents, Butch and Beverly Kittle, for instilling in me a love of reading, words, and books.

2. My supportive sister Monica, her husband Rick, and my smart, funny niece and nephew. Amy and Nathan never cease to amaze and inspire me with their creativity.

3. Lisa Bankoff, the best agent an author could ever dream of having. She has enriched my life in many ways beyond our professional relationship and introduced me to a new reason to be happy: heated mattress covers. (Life changing!)

4. Daniel Kirschen and Tina Wexler, also at ICM, for their expertise and efforts on my behalf.

5. Rebecca Frazer, dream editor, at Sourcebooks Jabberwocky; thank you for your passion and belief in Hannah and her world.

6. Todd Stocke, Aubrey Poole, Kristin Zelazko, Kelly Barrales-Saylor, Gretchen Stelter, and so many others in my Sourcebooks family, for your loving shepherding of this book into the world.

7. Dr. Diana G. Ackerly, who helped me understand bulimia and its treatment.

8. Bill Glisson (best boss I ever had), then principal of the Miami Valley Middle School, who let me travel with him and eight students for three weeks in Ghana that altered my life.

9. Sharyn November, editor extraordinaire, who wrote to me after reading *The Kindness of Strangers*, asking if I'd ever considered writing for a younger audience because she loved Jordan's and Nate's voices. At the time, I hadn't. This is all your fault. :-)

10. All of my former students at Centerville High School and the Miami Valley School, for challenging me, inspiring me, and teaching me as much as I ever taught you. I'd like to especially thank the MVS students who participated in the daily "Reasons to Be Happy" list on my whiteboard. You'll find many of your contributions in this book. Special love and thanks to Ellen, Libbi, and Claire.

11. Brooklyn, where I lived while writing this book. Beloved borough, you too altered my life.

12. Rachel Moulton, amazing friend and writer, first and last reader of all manuscripts. Thank you for believing in this story when I had stopped. And for the rock story. And for all the lattes. And

for seeing some reeeeally bad movies with me and still calling me friend.

13. The Antioch Writers' Workshop, for over a decade now of inspiration and community.

14. Culture Works, for two sustaining individual artist fellowships.

15. My incredible tribe of family—aunts, uncles, cousins, Nana— and cherished friends, both near and far. I am lucky.

About the Author

Katrina Kittle's reasons to be happy include:

1. her overflowing garden in Dayton, Ohio,

2. her fat cat, Joey,

3. coffee,

4. dark chocolate,

5. zombie movies, and

6. starting every morning in her writing office, doing what she loves most

She once had a goat under her bed in Ghana. She is the author of four other novels. You can visit her website at www.katrinakittle.com.